TRUTH 1

A JOURNEY TO FULFILLING RELATIONSHIPS

ALETHEA TAYLOR

TRUTH BE TOLD

A JOURNEY TO FULFILLING
RELATIONSHIPS

by

ALETHEA TAYLOR

Alethea Taylor, LLC
Philadelphia, PA

ISBN (Paperback): 9781733445207

Library of Congress Control Number: 2019920974

Printed in The United States

Alethea Taylor, LLC
Philadelphia, PA 19111-4567
www.AletheaTaylor1@outlook.com

Visit the author's website at www.AletheaTaylor.com

CONTENTS

PREFACE

Newly single after 20+ years and re-entering the dating arena, I was shocked to find that the rules, roles, the way the game was played, and the do's and don'ts of dating were now so confusing, shocking, and twisted. After dating a guy for a few months, I realized that he wasn't what I wanted at all. However, I continued with the relationship stubbornly ignoring the red flags that popped up like stop signs everywhere I looked. When the relationship did end, I was angry with myself for wasting my precious time with a man who didn't possess the characteristics I desired and for staying in a one-sided relationship.

I began to ask myself tough questions about why would I pursue, engage in, and continue with a relationship (whether platonic or romantic) with someone incapable of meeting my needs and desires. Logically, I knew better than to keep moving forward with it, yet I found myself constantly compromising my standards, which left me overwhelmingly dissatisfied with the relationship/friendship. I was always bringing our relationship issues to his attention and focusing on his inability to meet my expectations. This experience was more than empty, I had sucked the straw in the glass dry.

During this time, I realized I had many female family members, friends, co-workers, and acquaintances experiencing these same soul-searching conversations with themselves. They wanted to share their frustrations about their relationships with men. They wanted to tell me what their men did wrong, what they weren't doing, how inadequate they were, and how miserable their men made them feel. I saw them running in the same hamster wheels by hanging onto relationships, coping with men who cheated and engaged in unacceptable activities, and I saw women who stayed in relationships they neither needed or wanted.

I began to ask women to give me one sentence that summed up what they wish they'd done differently in their relationships. I told them to be as honest and candid as possible. Not only did the floodgates open, they exploded. By asking them to think about what they would have done differently, and then sharing their thoughts with me, I was forcing them to do some uncomfortable self-reflection and self-assessment. I wanted them to take responsibility for their part in the failure of the relationship and identify their brokenness, but more importantly, I wanted them to speak their TRUTH by digging into that dark, secret place of shame and get it all out because to do so was freeing, cleansing, liberating, and powerful.

These women were willing to share their truths. Their words and emotions conveyed through those words inspired me to write this book. I believe that when women share their relationship stories, they realize they're not alone. Just when you think your story is the worst imaginable, others come forward to share experiences and stories similar to yours. They describe how they survived negative relationships and how they battled through the fear that often prevented them from moving forward instead of embracing the experiences as valuable growth opportunities, learning opportunities, and discovery opportunities.

As much as we may want something to stay the same, change is inevitable, and ongoing self-evaluation is imperative. A desire for something different, for something more, for something meaningful, requires action. If you want to change your life, if you're searching for something better, you must do things differently and not allow fear to stop you. Be true to yourself. Know what you want in a man and what you want from a relationship. Don't be afraid to expect, and yes, **demand** those things. By doing so, you're taking a step in the right direction—embracing change rather than cowering from it.

ACKNOWLEDGMENTS

Giving praises to my **Lord and Savior, Jesus Christ**, from whom all blessings flow. Without Him, I can do nothing, but with Him all things are possible. I'm grateful for His love and for providing me everything I needed to give birth to this project. Thank you, Lord. I love you, Lord.

To my mother, **Nancy**, I love you dearly. Thank you for instilling in me the confidence to do whatever I set my mind to. You convinced me that the only person that could ever stop me from reaching my goals was me. Thank you, Mom, for being a strong, positive female influence in my life and for demonstrating how to persevere every day. Thank you for being my rock, my support, my cheerleader, and for believing in me, sharing your knowledge with me, and pushing me to do all I could do to fulfill my greatest potential. I thank you for loving me beyond measure and showing me how to love myself completely. I love you for always being willing to help and support me regardless of the situation. I find so much joy in knowing that you believe in me, that you continue to speak life over me, and encourage me to keep going. Most of all, Mom, thank you for being my mother, my friend, my comfort, and my security. I love you infinity times infinity!

To my late father, **James**, I'm proud to call you my father. You were a great father and the first man I saw who demonstrated the love of Christ to your family, your friends, and to all you knew or crossed your path. You were a true man of God. You supported me, loved me, and was always there for me. You also loved me beyond measure so that I, in turn, learned to love myself and know my worth. I miss you, Dad. I love you and carry you in my heart every day. I'm grateful to God for the many years we had together and most of all, I'm thankful to God for giving me a wonderful father like you!

To my sister, **Melinda,** my number one fan. I wouldn't be where I am today, nor could I have achieved what I have without your love and your support. You're my sister, my best friend, and I love you dearly! When I get weary, you push me, you pour your soul into mine, you speak life over me, you pray for me, and when my resources ebb, you make sure I have what I need. You're the epitome of selflessness. I'm your big sister, but you protect me. There's nothing you wouldn't do for me. You want only the greatest for me, not the best but the greatest, which you demonstrate with actions. Thank you. You love me wholeheartedly, and I love you more than words could ever express. I pray that God continues to bless you above and beyond just as He has blessed me above and beyond when he made you my sister!

To my brother, **Blain,** thank you for your love, your support, and your persistence in pushing me to finish this book. You often asked, "What's up with the book?" or "What's going on with the book?" You don't know how your words kept me on track. When distractions tried to block my way and prevent me from moving forward with this project, you were there with your questions. You didn't know it, but you kept me pushing on. You'll never know how much that meant to me, so thank you for believing in me. I love you dearly.

To my two beautiful and intelligent nieces, **Jada and Jordyn**—you're both the reason I started writing again and was inspired to continue completing my first book. Thank you! You make me want to be the best me I can possibly be. You're both my inspiration. I love you dearly.

Thank you to my four-legged baby boy, my "son" **Keno**. I'm grateful to you for the walks and time you demanded and needed. It's because of you that I wrote some of the best chapters of this book during our quiet times at the park. You bring joy to my life every day. Mommy loves you so much!

Creative credit to **Melinda**, my sister, for the design idea for the book cover, your ability to hear my heart, and to creatively develop the vision for an astonishing cover. You get me, you understand me, and more importantly, your idea completely captured the spirit of the book. Thank you for everything you do for me and for lending your gifts to the book cover.

To my illustrator, **Diona,** thank you for bringing the vision and the book cover design to life, which brought me to tears. Your design talent helped create the perfect book cover. I'm thankful for your talents and services.

To my videographer, **Cameron**, thank you for your creativity in delivering both a powerful and inspirational book trailer.

To my editors, **Kathie and Diana**, I am grateful to you both for your help editing this book. Your assistance and counsel were immeasurable; thank you!

Lastly, there are so many other **friends** and **family** members who continue to support and encourage me. To those of you who, throughout the birth of this book, cheered me on, believed in me, encouraged me, and were willing to help me see this project through to completion, thank you! To my New Taylor Made Committee Members, thank you for your work and dedication in sharing the news of the book with the world, and for your continued support and commitment to future projects. I'm so grateful for your help, support, and love. I've been blessed with the greatest support system anyone could wish for.

1 Thessalonians 5:11 *"Therefore encourage one another and build each other up, just as you are already doing."*

INTRODUCTION

"He did this."

"I can't believe him."

"OMG, this man is impossible."

"Guess what he did now."

"I'm so mad at him."

"He hurt me!"

What do you look for in a relationship? For that matter, what is a relationship? What are your expectations for the other person in this relationship? What is love? Define love? Is it fair to say that almost everyone defines love the same way? Do we? Is love an integral part of our relationships? Can we define a loving relationship?

The human yearning for love is natural. To love one another is normal. However, to be loved in return by just one person can be something very magical. Our desire to find that special person can be overwhelming. Wanting to be in a loving relationship, to share our lives with someone special, to start families, or to have a special friend or person in our lives is an innate, natural desire. However, the instinct that fuels our desire to find and be with someone can be overwhelming, particularly if that connection doesn't happen as quickly as we hope. Have you ever wanted something so badly that you were overwhelmed by a sense of sorrow? Such feelings can elicit knee-jerk reactions in certain stressful situations, lead us to make hasty, ill-conceived decisions, or take actions that may not be in our best interests.

Have you ever heard someone say she was tired of waiting to meet someone, or that she'd given up hope of meeting someone special? Did she complain that she was depressed because she hadn't met "the one" and had settled for the person she was with because she didn't believe the special person she so badly desired would ever come along? There are so many different thoughts, doubts, and beliefs that can ignite feelings of deep depression, desperation, and despair. They cause us to rush into hasty decisions that may feel or look right in the moment, but ultimately make us feel even worse in the end. Part of the problem is that often our desire is more powerful than our common sense. It clouds our ability to see someone for who they are and leaves us incapable of making good relationship choices.

We spend so much time pointing fingers, being angry, and feeling sad and depressed when relationships don't work out, we completely overlook how much better off we were when we were waiting for the right person to come along. We don't stop to consider that we should never have settled for the person we're with and are blind to the blessings we receive when a bad relationship ends in a breakup.

TRUTH BE TOLD | ALETHEA TAYLOR

There are many things that could have fractured the relationship—the demons that were exposed, arguments that revealed bitter truths, violent outbursts that happened once too often, the litany of derogatory names, the many times he disrespected you, the flood of cheating revelations you endured—any one of those discoveries may have been your "last straw"! Any of those things may have been just what you needed to see that person for who they always were and give you the courage and motivation you needed to leave, to stand up and speak out, to push onto greatness, to ignite your desire for more, and find room in your life for the *right* person.

Sometimes, events in our relationships—even bad events—lead us to something wonderful, things that we might never have otherwise achieved, sought, or pursued. Sure, we feel pain and betrayal at the moment. We experience disappointment, sadness, and depression for a while, but we can't allow ourselves to flounder in that dark, angry place forever.

It's so easy to point fingers at other people and blame them for fracturing the relationship, but if we're honest with ourselves, we have to ask, "What part did I play in this breakup? Did we have a choice? Were our choices taken away from us? Did we refuse to make choices?" We have to honestly assess whether the happiness or despair within the relationship was actually based on what our partner did or didn't provide. What part of our happiness depends on someone else making us happy, and what part of our happiness is a result of our actions? What do *we* own?

While each relationship is unique in its own right, women seem to have come to a universal conclusion regarding men. So very often, I hear women bash men for not being "good people". They make generalizations like, "Men aren't worth shit!" but is that a true assessment? Is it fair to categorize *all* men so negatively? Certainly, some men warrant that label, and rightfully so. However, is it possible that many men are unjustly categorized because of the women's actions (or the lack thereof)?

Could it be that the "monsters" we see in men evolved from the actions and inactions of the women? Did we contribute to creating these Frankensteins we criticize? Are we willing to reflect on our past and current relationships—casual, serious, and even our one-night stands—and admit our role in the failure, demise, or negative outcomes of our relationships with men? As women, what was our part in the situation? Did we fuel the emotional shipwreck that sank our relationships?

Can we be honest with ourselves? Are we? Should we be willing to peel back all the layers and reveal what we contributed to the relationship? To look at the terrible things with the same unbiased eye that we use to analyze the good. Did we do anything at all?

How did *our* actions influence some of the negative experiences that caused us to decide that, "All men are dogs," or that, "Men aren't worth shit?"

If we are really up to the challenge of exposing ourselves to the role we played in our relationships, we can change our paths. We can be the voice of reason or a guardian angel for someone else by helping them avoid the same mistakes we already made.

Do we accept or settle into relationships because we surrendered our hope or expectations of ever having anything more? Not more in terms of quantity, but in terms of quality. Do we believe that we deserve to be respected, honored, and treasured? Do we believe that our bodies are temples of God? Do we believe that with everything we're willing to give, we deserve the same or more in return? Do we love ourselves? We make sacrifices every day, but should those sacrifices lead to defeated relationships? God wants us to live an abundant life, to experience the richness of living, loving, and the feeling of joy along the way. Have you ever been in a relationship that left you feeling lonelier than you were when you were single? Is that *really* the relationship you want?

When you look back on some of your past relationships, are there things you wish you had done differently? Are there things you wish you had the strength and courage to do? As you reflect, can you admit that you were unable to see what was going on because the situation had completely swallowed you?

Conversely, were there times that you knew exactly what was making you unhappy, but you decided to ignore it and, in retrospect, wish you hadn't turned a blind eye? Of course, hindsight is always 20/20, but when you do have the opportunity to start over, do you take the more powerful route you envisioned in your reflection, or do you find yourself repeating the same relationship with a new player?

Something isn't quite right when we feel like we're living a "groundhog" relationship—randomly popping in and out of different holes but always seeing the same scenery. When do we take that first step toward change, if not for us, for someone else? Are we brave enough to do a self-inventory and face ourselves in the mirror? Are we strong enough to take note of our experiences and let them become our testimonies and share our enthusiasm for influencing future relationships and encouraging others?

This book brings together the stories of women's experiences and their truths as they relate to several types of relationships. The stories aren't those of any one person, rather they are a compilation of stories for every woman. As you read their stories, examine yourselves and be honest. It's a very liberating exercise, but more importantly, it's empowering and leads to hope and the determination to make changes to better yourself and inspire others. So free yourself, reclaim your power, and recognize your choices. Tomorrow starts with you!

What's **your** Truth to Be Told?

CHAPTER ONE

Toni

I Believed It Was Love

Roses are red, violets are blue, I did whatever this man told me to do! I loved Kevin so much. I loved him through everything. Whatever he did to me, with me, without me, it all came back to me loving him.

One of my girlfriend's held epic get-high sessions at her house. I loved attending those because you could hang out with people without judgment. Most of the time we spent the evening smoking marijuana, talking shit, and solving the problems of the world. For some reason, marijuana stimulated our brains and we got into some deep conversations as if we were rocket scientists. It was the funniest shit ever because we definitely weren't that smart.

The night I met Kevin, there were about thirty of us in her small house, which was a little more than usual, so we were really packed in. We started in the basement, but then some people drifted off into other rooms in the house to do some additional drugs. Some drank, some did cocaine, others popped pills, and a whole bunch of other shit. I made my way through the house, checking out what was going on and noticed Kevin sitting with a few men snorting cocaine in the living room. For some reason, I stood and watched them doing their thing for a minute or two before Kevin noticed me and asked me to join them. I didn't hesitate and snorted, laughed, and joked with the group, but my focus was on Kevin. Before the night was over, we exchanged phone numbers and went our separate ways.

Two months passed. I never called him, and he never called me, but then one Saturday night I was headed to a sports bar to meet some friends. When I entered, I spotted Kevin drinking at the bar with some buddies. We locked eyes and he immediately came over to talk to me. We spent the entire evening together and when we left the bar, we headed for his place. That was the best night I ever had. This man made love to me like he hadn't had sex in years. He couldn't get enough of me! When I woke up the next morning, I felt excited and sexually satisfied. I felt like I was in love. We spent the entire morning and afternoon together snorting cocaine and fucking. Honestly, it was the best time I'd had with a man in years.

Then I had to fuck it up by asking him to get me something to eat. I remember feeling so hungry after all our fucking. This was unusual because when I snorted cocaine, food was the furthest from my mind. But we'd been at it for so long I was hungry, so I asked, "Can you get me something to eat?". Kevin said, "Bitch, please, I don't have any money to feed you". This was the first danger sign that hinted of what lurked beneath the surface, but somehow, it was a turn on. Instead of jumping up and telling him never to call me a bitch, I actually thought it was funny and laughed. I convinced myself that he meant no harm, that it was just the way he talked, his lingo. Besides, the least I could do was buy the food. After all, he supplied the cocaine.

I got out of bed and walked to the nearest store in the cold because neither one of us had a car. Kevin didn't offer to walk with me. When I got back, I barely stepped through the door before he snatched the bags and grumbled that I'd taken too long to return. Again, I stayed silent, ignoring yet another blatant warning sign screaming in my mind. My instincts were on full alert, but I simply chose to ignore them because I wanted to be with Kevin. Although I wanted to respond to his attitude, I didn't. That day was the beginning of a rollercoaster relationship ride of shameful, degrading, and abusive experiences.

As our relationship progressed, most of the time I became the supplier for everything we needed. As long as Kevin fucked me good and spent some time with me, I allowed myself to further sink under his spell. I couldn't control myself. I was completely intoxicated by this man and my loss of control was the beginning of the end of me as I knew myself. So often I ask myself why I continued this toxic relationship. Kevin had nothing of value to offer me—no job, no money, no car. He was always bouncing in and out of jail, he still lived with his mother, and he was a drug addict and a thief who'd do anything for his next fix. Was someone like him really the best I could do?

What I chose to ignore was that Kevin was only a decent human being when he wasn't high from cocaine or heroin. Or at least that's the lie I told myself. I found myself making all sorts of excuses for his lifestyle. I believed he didn't have a job because he was socially disadvantaged. It was difficult for a black man to get work and that white men were always trying to hold a brother down. I thought not having his father in his life was the root of all of his misfortunes, even though Kevin had a hard-working, loving mother who provided everything for him and his brother. His brother was the total opposite—a hardworking, straitlaced dude who was a well-liked, law-abiding citizen. I thought, surely his mother must have loved his brother more than she loved my man. What else could have caused Kevin to turn out the way he did? I decided right then that I was going to love him. I thought if I showed him the love I assumed he never received, if I took care of him, and I was sure that if I gave him all I had to give, he'd straighten up and become the perfect man.

What a joke! More on myself than anyone else. I had no influence over this man, no control, but his power over me increased to the point where I became his puppet. Kevin was a controlling man. He wanted what he wanted, when he wanted it, and I better be ready to jump to his command, which I did. Whenever we spent time together, it was always laced with cocaine and other drugs. Often, things got crazy. One night, we were in his mother's basement getting high with a young woman. Kevin suddenly decided he wanted her to watch while we had sex. I was uncomfortable with this and told him so. He kept trying to convince me that it was no big deal. He said it would really turn him on for her to watch us have sex and that if I loved him, I'd do it. He began to kiss me passionately. He kissed my neck and squeezed my ass. I couldn't help get excited. He pulled up my t-shirt and removed my bra, and then his tongue traveled downward and settled ever so gently on one nipple. As he began to suck it, he used his fingers to firmly squeeze the other nipple. I could feel my pussy getting wet.

The high I was on from the drugs, the physical contact, and the immense pleasure he gave me caused me to completely forget about the woman in the room. It felt like the first time we had sex. Kevin unbuttoned my pants, stuck his hand in my panties, and pushed two fingers into my pussy. He thrust until I thought I was going to explode. While he was finger fucking me, his tongue traveled away from my breasts, down the middle of my stomach, over my belly button, and toward my pussy. I totally forgot we had an audience as I closed my eyes and gave myself up to the amazing sexual pleasure I was experiencing.

I was on the edge and almost ready to climax when Kevin suddenly withdrew his fingers from my pussy and slid them in again. I opened my eyes to see what interrupted my pleasure and realized the girl was on her knees sucking his dick and the fingers in my pussy that I thought were his, were hers. I was spread-eagle on the pool table while he stood close beside me. I slapped her hand away and shoved hard against Kevin's chest as I jumped off the table and started screaming at both of them, "What the fuck is this?" I lost it. I couldn't believe he'd do this to me, to us! No one had ever joined us while we were having sex, and I'd certainly never had a lesbian encounter before.

I didn't want to share Kevin and couldn't handle watching my man fuck another woman. I felt so disrespected and violated that I couldn't control my anger. I remember him telling me to calm down, but I continued to focus my rage on both of them. Suddenly, I felt a cool, refreshing breeze, the sensation you experience after popping a Tic Tac in your mouth. Little did I know at the time that the feeling I mistook for a cool, refreshing breeze was me being knocked out. I woke up with a bloody nose and a missing tooth. Instead of waking up angry because he hit me, I somehow convinced myself that I'd provoked him into hitting me—that I deserved it because I lost it. I yelled and screamed, spat and pointed my finger in his face. Hitting me was his way of bringing me back to reality the only way he knew how.

I told myself that if only I could learn to control myself, control my temper, control my reactions, Kevin wouldn't have to beat me. He only beat me because he loved me, and if I truly loved him, I'd do whatever he wanted. I knew he had an insatiable sexual appetite, which is what I loved about our relationship. We were always fucking! We enjoyed exciting sexual experiences because we did it anywhere and everywhere. I simply didn't realize that he had a desire to bring someone else into bed with us. If I loved him, regardless of my feelings, I should have been willing to please him any way I could. Anything less would be selfish. I created an impossible situation for him and he reacted the best way he could.

Although we got past that incident, Kevin never apologized, but I knew he was sorry. He tried to make it up to me by telling me that he wanted me to meet his father. I guess that was his way of making me feel "special". I'd heard many stories about his father, who wasn't the best father to Kevin. I wanted to see this man for myself. I constantly asked Kevin to introduce me to his father, but he only said, "I will". A couple of days after knocking me out, he said, "I want you to meet my father". He knew that would melt my heart. His mother said Kevin had never taken any woman to meet his father, so when Kevin told me I'd be meeting him, I knew he truly loved me and that I was the one!

Two weeks later, Kevin arranged a day for us to visit his father on a Saturday. I was looking forward to meeting his father and happy that Kevin was making more of an effort to see his father more. Over the past two years, they'd been working on rebuilding their relationship, and it appeared to be going well. His father had drifted in and out of Kevin's life because he was a drug user and he couldn't commit to being a father while his son was growing up, which was one more reason for me to love Kevin with all my being.

Saturday night finally came. Two hours before we were supposed to be at his father's house, I made sure I prepped and prepared my best outfit because I wanted to look my best when I met Kevin's father. I put on my nice red dress, a black jacket, loosened my hair from the rubber band to let it fall onto my shoulders, and applied my favorite perfume. I wanted to ensure I represented Kevin well and make a good impression on his father. When we got to his father's house, we chatted for a bit and then sat down to the wonderful dinner his father prepared for us. After dinner, we started to drink, smoke weed, and do a little cocaine. We were having a great time. But as usual, Kevin got horny and started to grab me, touch me, clutch me from behind, and grind on my ass. His father just laughed and said, "I can see why you're all over her, she's fine. Shit, my dick is hard".

We both laughed because "Pop", as he called him, had no filters. Any thought that came into his head would spew right out of his mouth. To stop any physical contact in front of his dad, I went to the bathroom. When I got back, I found them both whispering and laughing. I chalked it up to a private conversation, but I soon learned they were talking about me—my body and more specifically, my ass. I've always had a big ass, and most of the time I wore clothing that specifically concealed it, but my efforts weren't always successful. This particular night, I hadn't been able to hide my ass. They both encouraged me to take another drink and snort another line of cocaine. Of course, they didn't have to ask me twice because I was glad to.

Then Pop put on some music and we were all singing along with the music and dancing in the middle of the floor. The next thing I knew, Pop was close behind me, whispering in my ear, asking if he could see and feel my titties and ass. I pushed him hard and said,

"No!" Kevin quickly approached me and grabbed me by my throat. He said, "Bitch, don't you *ever* push my father. He only wanted to see your breasts and feel your ass, so what's the problem?" Did I hear him right? I was totally shocked. I was trying to gather my thoughts, but it was difficult because I was so high. Kevin went on to say that he wanted me to do something for him—he wanted me to let Pop see my body. I couldn't believe my ears, so I asked, "You want me to let your Pop see my body and touch it?"

He grabbed me by my throat and started to choke me while shouting and yelling, "I don't see what the problem is. I want you to do this for me. It will turn me on. I need you to do this for me!" I immediately thought about the last time I rejected his twisted sexual requests and the beating he gave me. My eyes filled with hot, salty tears as I quickly snorted another line of cocaine and backed up against the wall to prepare for what I was about to do. Kevin came and began to kiss me and tell me how much he loved me while his father watched. Kevin told me he wanted me to suck his dick. I dropped to my knees, unzipped his jeans, pulled out his dick, and started to suck it. His father sat forward in his chair, eyes bugging, and shouted, "Damn, yes, suck his dick!" As I continued to suck Kevin's dick, Kevin called his father over. The tears brimming in my eyes now streamed freely down my face. Kevin noticed me crying and grabbed my hair and yanked my head back hard until he looked me in the eyes. He told me to stop crying, dry my face, and do whatever his father wanted.

Pop approached me, took my hand, and led me to a reclining chair. Since I was wearing a dress, there was easy access for either of them to fuck me if they wanted. As I sat down, Pop instructed me to open my legs because he wanted to see my panties. I did as I was told. He told me to take them off, open my legs, and show him my pussy. I was struggling to hold back my tears as Kevin shouted, "Get her, Pop". Pop said, "I just want to eat your pussy. I haven't eaten any pussy in a long, long time. I just want to smell and taste a pussy!"

Pop began licking my pussy. He licked hard, pressing his whiskered face into my pussy harder and harder while Kevin watched laughing and cheering. At first, I tried not to think about what was happening. I didn't want to enjoy it, but then it started to feel so good that I couldn't stop my body from responding to the hot, wet stimulation. To make things worse, Kevin joined in and started rubbing my breasts. I was so confused to think I was participating in a threesome with Kevin and his father. This was a sick, dysfunctional experience, *but it felt so good!* Pop told me to turn over, get on my knees, and lean over the chair, which exposed my ass for his pleasure. Pop rubbed it, licked it, and then inserted three fingers into my ass while smacking my cheeks with his other hand. He was growing excited, and the more excited he became, the harder he thrust his fingers into my ass. Again, Kevin yelled, "Get it, Dad. Get all in there!" Once Pop finished licking my ass, he told me to get on my knees and suck his dick.

As soon as I hesitated, Kevin struck me on the back of my head with his fist and ordered me to do it and do it well, so I put Pop's dick in my mouth as far as it would go. I started to gag a little because I was trying to swallow his dick up to his balls, but I suppressed it for fear of getting knocked out again. As I sucked Pop's dick, Kevin fucked me from the back. I was crying, but the sad thing is that I wasn't crying solely because I didn't want to do it. I was crying because it felt so good! Once Kevin came, he told me to turn around so Pop could fuck me. Pop had me stand up, lean over the table, and then he fucked me from behind while telling me what a nasty bitch I was. He grabbed my hair and slapped my ass while Kevin whispered in my ear that I'd better enjoy it and cum. Pop made me cum quickly—something I didn't want to do. When Pop was ready to cum, he pulled out his dick and told me to hurry and suck it because he wanted to cum in my mouth and for me to swallow every drop. As he stuck his dick in my mouth, Kevin growled that I'd better swallow it all or he'd crack my face! Pop came in my mouth and I swallowed every drop of his cum, but by then I couldn't hold back my tears.

Kevin told me to get up and get myself together, so I did as I was told. I went to the bathroom and collected myself. While I was sitting on the edge of the tub trying to process what just happened, Kevin knocked on the door and came in to thank me for what I did for him. He said he was more in love with me now than he'd ever been before. He kissed me gently on the forehead and said, "I really do love you!" To hear this from my man, to hear that I pleased him and that he loved me more for it made me feel good in a sick, twisted way. I did what Kevin wanted and he was happy with me. I began to reconsider what happened. I convinced myself that the events of the evening hadn't been so bad. After all, I got immense pleasure from the encounter and I did cum, so it hadn't all been bad. In my weakness and desperate desire to please Kevin, this reasoning was my coping mechanism.

After the evening with his father, I felt like Kevin and I were growing closer. The love I felt for him deepened and I was excited to have a man who wanted to be with me. While I went to work each day, Kevin stayed home with his mother and waited for me to return. I made sure I called him before I left work every day to ask what he wanted for dinner. I stopped to get whatever he wanted to eat and pick up a bag of weed or cocaine on my way home. One Friday, I phoned him to see what he wanted, but there was no answer. I was surprised when he popped up where I worked twenty minutes later.

At that time, I worked for a popular store that sold the majority of designer eyewear in the area. I got paid every other Friday, but the Friday Kevin came to the store wasn't a payday for me. When he arrived, he was angry, agitated, and jumpy. He asked me for money. I tried to explain to him that I wouldn't get paid until next week and that I didn't have any money. I knew he needed a fix, but I had nothing to give him. He told me to take some money out of the store's register. I was terrified to take the money, but he told me it was no big deal. He told me I wouldn't get caught because there weren't any other employees in the store to see me take it. Reluctantly, I took a handful of twenties and tens from the register and gave it to Kevin without even counting it. Kevin still wasn't satisfied and wanted me to give him some glasses to sell on the streets. I went to the storage area, grabbed three pairs of Prada sunglasses, and gave them to him.

As I watched him leave, I got nervous. I felt guilty for stealing money and merchandise from the store. I had a drug habit too, but I never stole anything from the store before. While I thought about it a few times, I never acted on it. Now I was worried and anxious because I stole for him, but like always, my love for him outweighed my guilt. Yes, I know what I did was wrong, but I persuaded myself that I'd done it for a good reason. After all, Kevin didn't have any money. I didn't get caught that first time. Nobody noticed or questioned me about the shortage in my cash drawer, so I did it again, and again. This continued for two months before my regional director came to the store and informed me that management had noticed numerous cash shortages at my store and that the shortages only happened during my shifts, so I was fired.

I left the store feeling sad, shocked, and oddly thankful. I regretted that I'd been caught and lost my job, but I was thankful no one discovered the inventory I stole for side cash. I walked two blocks to the bus stop to meet Kevin. I hoped he'd greet me with a big hug and make everything better, but as I approached, he immediately knew from my demeanor and facial expression that something was wrong. He asked me what happened and when I told him that I'd been fired, he latched into a full-on assault. He kicked me multiple times. The first kick landed on my hip, and then others followed to my butt, my back, and knee. He was kicking with all his strength and rage. This took place at a public bus stop on a street corner with cars and people going by. He continued to kick me and shower me with insults like, "Dumb bitch! You so stupid. You ain't worth shit."

TRUTH BE TOLD | ALETHEA TAYLOR

I was so embarrassed, scared, and in pain. For some reason, I was shocked, as if a beating was something new, but I suppose it was because he was beating me in public. I tried to protect myself by blocking his kicks, but he thought I was trying to hit him back, so he grabbed me by the hair, and then my throat and started choking me. I fell to my knees begging him to stop, yelling, "You're going to kill me!" but he wouldn't stop. I heard people yelling, "Get off of her!" but no one had the courage to jump in and physically pull him off me. I heard a car pull up and a male voice yelled, "Get your fucking hands off her. You don't touch a woman!" Kevin responded, "Fuck you! Mind your own business!" The man replied, "This is my business".

The next thing I knew, the man jumped out of his car, grabbed Kevin, and threw him to the ground. When he tried to pick me up, Kevin jumped on his back and I fell to the ground. The man somehow got Kevin off his back and body-slammed him to the ground. This time he began to beat Kevin in the face, and with every punch, he screamed, "So, you like to beat on women, huh?" Finally, he stopped and asked if I was okay. When I nodded and said, "Thank you!", the man jumped into his car and sped off before two bike cops showed up. The witnesses told the cops what happened, and they handcuffed Kevin and took him away. Before they left, they asked me what happened and if he'd been beating me, but I wouldn't answer. It didn't matter because witnesses had provided enough evidence and Kevin was taken away.

Because I refused to go to the hospital, I was left to care for my injuries. The next day, I had a huge knot on my forehead, a bad cut under one eye, and bruises all over my body. Despite that, I wasn't worried about myself. I was worried about Kevin being in jail. He called me Saturday night, and, as usual, apologized profusely. He explained that he reacted that way because he'd snorted some cocaine and was simply out of his head. He begged me to forgive him because he hadn't been himself. It was the drugs. He told me he loved me, that he'd never do that to me again, and wanted to prove he could be the man I deserved. Gullible and desperate as I always was, I believed his actions were caused by the drugs, so I forgave him. I posted his bail Monday morning. We got past the incident—he didn't have to serve any time because it was a domestic incident and because I lied. I told the authorities that I attacked him and he'd been simply trying to stop me.

After losing my job, we went through a tough time. We were both unemployed. Well, I was unemployed, Kevin never had a job. We didn't have money for food, clothing, drugs—the basic everyday necessities. We were living with Kevin's mother. She let us stay in the basement for a few weeks before she told us we had to give her money for staying in her house and that we'd have to buy our own food because she couldn't support us any longer. We didn't know any way to get money other than to steal it. That was what Kevin did when I wasn't supplying enough for our needs. There were times he'd go out and steal so we could pawn the stuff to get money for what we needed.

I remember one time he broke into someone's house just so he could get some money to buy me sanitary napkins. No one got hurt in any of the burglaries he committed. Oh, he had to rough up some old people now and again, push and shove his mother, and smack around his uncle, and yeah, he broke his brother's jaw, but all-in-all, people weren't hurt all that bad. We had to survive, didn't we? We were both cocaine addicts. We had to have it. How many men broke into homes and stole for their woman? I bet not many, which is why he was so special to me. I loved him. But this time was different. Kevin decided that instead of stealing, he'd send me out to fuck men for money.

Again, another mind-blowing suggestion, or should I say, "demand" from Kevin, and yet again, I agreed to do something I didn't want to do. When he first presented his plan to me, I flat out told him I couldn't do it. He reminded me it wouldn't be the first time I'd fucked a man or men to get some drugs, and that this would be no different. I just shook my head and said, "No, no, no, I can't do it!" Kevin told me that if I didn't do what he asked he'd hurt my mother. She was a nurse and she worked the 3 pm-11 pm shift. She didn't get home most nights until midnight or later. Kevin swore that if I didn't do this, he'd wait in a bush, jump my mother, and rob her. You'd think that after hearing his threats toward my mother I'd leave him, but I didn't. I agreed to "a session" as Kevin called them because I didn't want him to hurt my mother and I knew he would if I didn't do what he asked or if I tried to leave him.

Kevin planned to put the word out on the street that he had a girl available on Friday night to fuck for whoever could pay. I was no stranger to the streets, bars, and drug houses in the area, and many of the local men knew who I was and had either fucked me already or wanted to fuck me for the first time. Finding men interested in paying money to fuck me wasn't difficult to do. Kevin traveled to bars and clubs and talked to men on street corners about how they could come to his mother's basement anytime Friday night to fuck me or engage in any other sexual activity that interested them. I prepared myself by taking a shower, putting on something nice, and used Kevin's mother's perfume to make sure I smelled good. I told Kevin I needed some drugs to help me through the evening even though I hoped no one would show up. He gave me some pills that soon helped me stop thinking about anything and numbed me for what was about to take place. If anything, the drugs made me horny and I was more than ready to fuck.

Around 8:30 pm, I was startled by someone banging on the basement door. Kevin rushed to open the door telling me over his shoulder to get ready, but I was hoping he was wrong. When he opened the door, three men stood there. As they entered the basement, and before Kevin could close the door, one of the men said, "No, don't close the door, there are more coming". All I could think was, *Wow*. I was still feeling the effects of drugs Kevin gave me. Music was playing and I was dancing. There were eight men in the basement. I hoped that only one had come for the fun and the others were just going to wait for him. However, to my surprise, when Kevin asked who was there to have fun, they all raised their hands, and someone shouted, "Let's get this show on the road!" Kevin responded, "Who's first? Twenty dollars. What's your pleasure?" One guy said, "I want my dick sucked!" The others laughed and told him to pull out his dick. He did as suggested. I looked at Kevin and he nodded for me to go ahead. The one thing I knew I was good at was sucking dick. I knew how to use my tongue on a dick to make a man cum fast, so I wasn't worried about having to suck this guy's dick for long. I moved over to the guy and took his dick in my mouth.

Just as I thought, he came in less than a minute. I was relieved it was over so quickly. Three more guys decided that they wanted the same thing and lined up for me to perform while the others watched. Kevin just sat in the corner and collected the money. After I finished with each of the four guys I sucked off, I asked for another pill to help numb me. When the fifth guy was up for his encounter, he said he wanted to fuck me. I hesitated, but Kevin quickly shouted. "Fifty dollars". The guy responded, "No problem", and tossed the money at Kevin. I lay down on the sofa and he came over and started fucking me. I might as well have been a blowup doll for all the regard he had for me. He thrust like an animal while the others watched and cheered him on.

The sixth and seventh guys also wanted to have sex. One made me lean over the sofa so he could fuck me from behind. When it was the other guy's turn, he wanted to sit in the chair and have me straddle him. Again, he was thrusting so hard he hurt me. I was nothing more than a hole to them, a whore, a piece of meat. Finally, I got to the last guy. Soon it would be over, but he turned out to be the worst of all. He patiently waited his turn while I serviced the others, but when Kevin asked, "What's your pleasure?" the man pulled out a stack of money and said, "I want to fuck her in her ass!" I immediately responded, "No! No way!" He got angry and yelled at Kevin, "I thought you

said whatever we wanted, we could get", Kevin
responded, "Yeah, you can. She'll do it, no problem.
Just give me a minute."

Kevin dragged me to the top of the stairs and
told me I'd better do what the man wanted. He quickly
reminded me that he'd fuck me up and go after my
mother if I didn't let the man fuck me in the ass.
Before I went back downstairs, I heard the men
laughing. The man who wanted to fuck me was telling
the others that he "Was going to fuck the shit out of
me, literally!" I dreaded doing this. I didn't want to get
fucked in the ass! But I went downstairs because I had
to consider my mother. I had to do this to keep her
safe! Before we got started, I told the man he needed
some lube. He said, "No, it'll be ok. I have something".
He made me lay down on the sofa ass up and I heard
him spit into his hands. When he tried to insert his dick
into my ass, it was unbelievably painful. He couldn't get
it in at first and he got angry. I tried to persuade him to
put it in my vagina instead, but the others encouraged
him to keep trying.

He finally pushed his dick into my ass. It was
agony. I wanted him to stop but he kept going. He
fucked me like a machine. I started to cry, but he kept
going. He came after about three minutes. When he
pulled out, I felt a rush of blood. I jumped up and ran
to the third-floor bathroom in pain and disgust. These
men had treated me like I wasn't even human and

Kevin was fine with that as long as he got his money. I was upstairs for twenty minutes before Kevin came to the bathroom not to ask me if I was ok, but to tell me that, *"We"* made some good money. The guy who fucked me in the ass paid one-hundred dollars. That, along with the money from the other men, meant we were on a roll. I told him I was glad it was over, and he reminded me that we still had the rest of the night and the following morning to make more money. I told him I couldn't do it and he punched me in the nose. It started bleeding and I began crying uncontrollably. Now I was bleeding from my nose and my ass. I couldn't believe what was happening to me.

Kevin told me if I wanted to eat and have a place to stay, I should be willing to have sex to get the money to pay for it. He gave me a line of cocaine to snort and it made everything better. I calmed down and the session continued into the early hours of the morning. When it was over, I had sex with twenty-six men that night. My body, my vagina, my ass, my breasts, and my mouth were all sore, nasty, and disgusting, but I kept things in perspective. We had a few hundred dollars and enough drugs to last for two days. We made so much money that we scheduled sessions for Saturday and Sunday, totaling three days. I fucked and sucked forty-eight men and two women that weekend. Over the next two weeks, I agreed to several sessions, and we made enough money to purchase a car, pay his mother for a month, and buy food and drugs. I was completely numb to the sex enslavement I endured. I simply convinced myself that there were many women who had sex for money to take care of their families and that's what I was doing. It wasn't so bad. At least, that was the mantra I repeated to make myself believe that my degradation was justified.

After about two months, we got back on our feet and were doing well. One evening, while driving home from a party, the police stopped us for a broken taillight. We only recently bought the car with some of the money from the sessions. We were aware that the car had a broken taillight but forgot to take care of it. The cop approached the car and I was worried because we both had been drinking and smoking marijuana at the party, so we weren't too coherent. The cop asked for our registration and insurance information, but it was obvious that Kevin was slow to respond and couldn't seem to remember where to find the information. I tried to whisper that it was in the side of the driver's door, but he wasn't listening to me. The cop then asked, "Sir, have you been drinking?"

When Kevin didn't answer, the cop asked again, "Sir, have you been drinking?" Kevin still didn't respond so the cop asked him to step out the car. When he did, he stumbled and it was obvious to the cop that Kevin had been drinking and shouldn't have been driving. Again, the cop asked for the registration and insurance information. I pointed to the side of the open door and when Kevin reached for the information, several bags of cocaine fell out with the documents. The cop looked at the bags. I stared in surprise and Kevin looked, then turned his head away. The cop reached down and picked up the bags. He asked Kevin, "Are these yours?" Kevin immediately said, "No, they're hers!" and he pointed at me. The cop asked me if the bags were mine. I stumbled over my words not because the bags were mine, but because I couldn't believe Kevin had told the cops that the bags were mine. I was dumbfounded, so I just sat in silence. The cop arrested us both. I stayed in jail for one week, but Kevin was released the next day. When I was asked about the bags of cocaine, I never denied they were mine. The car was registered in my name so I assumed they'd believe that the drugs were mine, too.

At first, I wasn't angry because I understood why Kevin told the cop the drugs were mine. He's spent too much time in jail and if he was arrested again, particularly for drugs, he'd do some hard time, so I went along with his story and took the rap for the drugs. Since I'd never been arrested before I thought I'd get a slap on the wrist and probation because I was a first-time offender, but the judge wasn't having any of that. I was sentenced to two years and three months for possession of a controlled substance. I was in complete shock. I couldn't believe that I'd been sentenced to serve time, particularly for something I didn't do and for drugs that weren't even mine. My family was so disappointed in me. I didn't even need to admit to my family that the drugs were Kevin's, they automatically assumed the cocaine was his and that I was taking the rap for him. They all knew I did drugs, but they thought Kevin was a no-good bum and that I'd do ANYTHING for him. Lying about the drugs being mine to save his ass was something I was conditioned to do.

When I first began my sentence, I was angry and sad. I didn't know how to handle being locked up. I had never been to jail, despite some of the things I did out in the streets. For the first month, I cried my eyes out. I didn't see anyone for a month and I was desperately missing Kevin. However, after about seven weeks, he came for a visit. He started visiting me twice a month. I was happy when he came to see me because I couldn't talk to him much the rest of the time as he didn't have a working cell phone. He used my cell phone for a while until my sister stopped paying the bill. She couldn't afford to put money on my books in jail and maintain a cell phone that wasn't being used, or that she thought wasn't being used. Five months into my sentence, Kevin's visits dropped from twice a month, to once a month, and then once every two months. Eventually, he stopped visiting altogether.

Now I was angry and deeply depressed. I felt like an idiot. Here I was in jail for something I didn't do while he was getting on with his life. He said he loved me but he sure wasn't showing me any love especially since I was in here for him. I was serving time for him. Now that's love!

My family and friends supported me while I was locked up. They visited, wrote me letters, and put money on the books so I could buy basic things I needed like underwear, toothpaste, soap, etc. When they visited, they told me what was happening on the outside and whether they'd seen or heard from Kevin. One Saturday afternoon, my sister came to see me and told me she'd heard that Kevin was living with his ex-girlfriend and she thought they were expecting a baby. She was concerned about telling me but thought I needed to know. I was utterly crushed. The agony I felt was unbearable. I couldn't believe it! I had no way of contacting Kevin to ask him if what my sister told me was true. My last three months in prison were miserable. I felt like a fool for surrendering my life for someone like him. But for some perverse reason, I still loved him, and I just couldn't control my feelings. The day I was released, all I wanted to do was to see him, talk to him, and find out if what I heard was true. I knew where his ex-girlfriend lived but I didn't have a car. I begged my sister to drive me, but she refused. I called my cousin and asked her to drive me to my girlfriend's house. It was a lie, but the only way I could get someone to drive me to see him.

When we got to the house, I didn't get out of the car right away. I knew I shouldn't have come to the woman's house, but I had to know what was going on. I hesitantly confessed to my cousin that this wasn't my friend's house. It was Kevin's ex-girlfriend's house. She was furious that I'd want to do something so foolish. She said I shouldn't knock on the door of a strange woman to chase a worthless man. She said the woman would have every right to shoot me if she wanted and tell the police it was self-defense because I'd come after her in her house.

Stubborn as always, I got out of the car and slowly walked across the street to the house. My heart was pounding—not because I was scared, but because I was afraid that everything my family and friends had been telling me would turn out to be true. Kevin was there living a life with someone else, starting a family with someone else while he left me to rot in jail. I knocked on the door and nearly fell back a step when the door opened. I wasn't prepared for what I saw. Kevin opened the door with a child in his arms. My heart dropped and tears filled my eyes. He was shocked to see me. It took a few minutes before he asked, "When did you get out?"

"I got out today. I heard you were living here." Then I asked, "Whose baby are you holding?" Without apology, he replied, "This is my son. I'm sorry you had to find out like this. I wanted to talk to you and explain the situation." I shook my head in disbelief and slowly backed away. I can't explain the depths of the pain I felt in my heart. I was weak from a barrage of feelings that felt like steel bands crushing my very soul— betrayal, abandonment, and most of all, stupidity. I thought of everything he'd done to me and the degrading things he forced me to do. I remembered the beatings, the pain, and despair. The memories overwhelmed me to the point where I lost control of my body. My legs began to shake and gave way. I collapsed to the ground. Can you even begin to imagine how devastating it is to lose control of your body? You want to know the craziest thing of all? I STILL LOVED HIM! I was drowning in a sea of mixed feelings and devastation. Not only had I lost control of my body, but now I was losing my mind. When I got back to the car, my cousin was crying. She saw the pain on my face and knew he wasn't worth the suffering he caused me.

The day I got out of prison was supposed to be a joyful day, a cause for celebration. Instead, it turned out to be worse than any of the time I spent in prison.

My cousin was going to take me to my mother's house where my friends and family had gathered for my release party, but first I had to pull myself together. I didn't want my family to see me in my distressed condition. We stopped at my cousin's house so I could collect myself before we went to my mother's house for the celebration. When we got there, I put on a brave face but she knew I was pretending and wasn't as happy as I should have been. Later that night after the guests left, my mother took me to the back deck and told me she knew something was wrong. She said she'd bet her last dollar that it involved Kevin. She started crying and begged me to leave him before I was seriously hurt. She began apologizing and repeating that she was sorry. I didn't understand why she was apologizing to me so I didn't interrupt her and let her speak. She started telling me that over the years, I watched her stay in relationships after many of her boyfriends would physically harm her, slap her around, kick her, and beat her in front of her children. She went on to explain that she watched my grandmother suffer the same beatings from men and how she endured the abuse. Then I watched my mother endure the same physical and mental abuse, which allowed the cycle to be passed down to me.

We believed it was okay to stay with a man who was physically and emotionally abusive because we didn't recognize or understand that what we suffered had nothing to do with love. The women in our family had come to believe that we triggered the violence and verbal abuse from our men, that although they loved us, it was our fault because we pushed them to the breaking point. My mother further explained that this toxic generational cycle must stop now! It took her a lifetime to realize that love should never manifest in physical, mental, or verbal abuse. She didn't want me to waste any more time learning the same lesson.

I never considered my situation as she spoke, but I knew there was truth to her words. She apologized again for subjecting me to her bad decisions and not setting the right example for me. While she made bad decisions for a long time, she wanted better and more for me. My mother looked straight into my eyes and said, "I love you and I want better for you, but you have to want better for yourself too and find the strength to let go!" She'd told me this before, but for some reason, this time her words resonated in my mind. She was right. Only I could decide that I wanted and deserved better for myself. Knowing that my mother was able to accomplish this, I knew I could too.

Truth Be Told, I allowed my deep-rooted insecurity and low self-esteem to trap me into making decisions I'm ashamed of. I was a grown woman with a mind of my own, but I reverted to a helpless child unable to stop the damage I inflicted on myself for what I foolishly believed was love. While Kevin was an evil and abusive manipulator, I was driven by a desperate need for love. The poor choices of men in my life were never the problem. I was my own worst enemy without the strength to face the truth that scarred me like the many bruises I received from my beatings. I lied, stole, cheated, and defiled myself FOR A MAN! I was so starved for attention I latched onto it like a drowning swimmer and endured debasement, humiliation, and pain to hang onto it.

No, I never asked to be beaten, and no, it wasn't my fault. I know now that it's not a woman's fault when a man puts his hands on her because such men are the ultimate cowards. I realize now that instead of feeling ashamed of Kevin hitting me, beating me, and humiliating me, I should have told someone what was going on or sought assistance from the many resources available to women in abusive relationships, such as battered women's organizations, churches, and the authorities. When you're in survival mode, it's hard to focus on seeking help when you're in such a terrible situation. To Kevin, I was nothing more than a commodity to be used for profit in human trafficking. I was one of countless women and girls subjected to such sexual horror on a daily basis. But I always had to power to stop it. I only had to find it within myself.

Truth Be Told, I didn't love myself enough to be able to love someone else. Instead of trying to love someone through their troubles, I should have first examined my own issues. When I looked in the mirror, I didn't see the problems I needed to work on. However, the painful experiences of my relationship with Kevin forced me to take a cold, hard look at myself. Sometimes to face the truth, we must fall to our lowest point. We have to suffer before we can learn how to pull ourselves up. I'd always chased love. What I didn't realize was that I always had it. It was there within me all this time.

Truth Be Told, it was a struggle for me to learn how to accept that love. With the help of friends, family, and hearing similar stories like mine, I was finally able to journey the long road to sobriety and self-love. Fortunately, I'm not the woman I was when I was with Kevin. I'm no longer a doormat for anyone! I allowed disregard, disrespect, and violence into my life and it beat me down. I was incapable of defending myself—but no more! From now on, I will stand up and love *me* enough so that I'll never have to sacrifice myself to love a man more.

CHAPTER TWO

Cassandra

Married and Miserable

I wore blinders because I wanted to be married and to have a family. What I found was that I was more miserable as a married woman than I'd ever been as a single woman.

I'm finally married. I have everything I've ever wanted—the house, the cars, the job, the money, the man, and children of my own. It's like a fairy tale, except that I'm not in love with my husband! I respect him, admire his drive and his great upbringing, and his values and beliefs related to taking care of his wife and family. He has all the qualities I hoped my dream man would possess, but still, I'm not in love with him. I love him as a person. He's a good man, but **Truth Be Told**, we don't have the deep connection that a couple truly in love should share—the kind of connection that leads them to take the plunge into marriage and happily ever after.

Maybe we expect too much when we're younger. We get swept up by starry-eyed romanticism straight from the plot of a movie. We yearn for our knight in shining armor, but those soft-focus fantasies rarely translate to the hard reality of life. They linger like whispering ghosts fostering disappointment, envy, and the eternal, "Why me?" when we see that what we desperately desire touches everyone except us.

Truth Be Told, I wanted a husband, and I was tired of waiting. He was a willing and eager participant, so I went for it. I had everything else I wanted in life. I worked for a wonderful global company, and I loved my job even though it required frequent travel to eleven states across the country. The problem was that the job impeded my ability to establish any meaningful relationships. I simply didn't have time to get to know anyone. For seven years, I traveled and worked hard, but loneliness rooted within me like a tenacious weed and planted a deep sadness. It began to negatively affect me both physically and mentally. I felt increasingly despondent and depressed. Wherever I looked, I saw couples and families. Yes, I was jealous. I wanted what seemed so effortless for others. It didn't matter that there could have been more lurking beneath those shiny surfaces. I'd reached a point where I abandoned all hope of marriage and a family and envisioned a future where I was old and alone. I prayed constantly. I asked God to send me a man, but weeks turned into months, and months turned into years. Still, there was no man in my life. Yes, I met men here and there, but nothing long-term or substantial ever came from our dates. It seemed the more people I was surrounded by, the lonelier I felt.

Sex was a different matter. I had several good sexual encounters but far too many of them left me feeling dissatisfied and sorry that I'd shared my body with such losers. What was meant to be a temporary release only fueled my sense of isolation and disconnection. I felt anonymous, invisible to the world. As a result, I buried myself in my work and purposely took on as many projects as I could. I worked long hours so I could stay busy and exhaust myself. When I arrived home at the end of the day, I barely had enough energy to shower, eat, and crawl into bed. I wanted to be sure I could silence the voices of regret and longing for a relationship. On the weekends, when I didn't have to work, all I did was shop! Shopping was the one thing that brought me immense pleasure. It helped briefly distract me from the loneliness and mask the pain resonating through my heart and soul.

I recall leaving for work one day. When I left the house, the sadness I skillfully concealed found its way to my face. It must have replaced the fake smile I usually wore because one of my co-workers, Katie, noticed and asked if I was all right. I shrugged and gave a weak, "Yes, I'm ok". She looked at me for a minute and then invited me to have a drink with her after work so we could talk. I hesitated, but she insisted. She said she was meeting some other friends and her brother who was in town for the holidays. I thought nothing of her mentioning that her brother would be there. I was too busy feeling sorry for myself. Maybe going for a drink *was* a good idea. One or two drinks might help numb my pain, so I agreed to go. After all, it beat going home alone on a Friday night. My game plan was to have a couple of drinks and then go home. That way, if anyone asked, I could say I had some fun Friday night instead of admitting that I stayed home alone watching television.

When we arrived at the bar, it was somewhat crowded, which was typical for a Friday night. Katie led the way to a nearby table where three people were seated—two men and one woman. The men weren't anything special, just average looking. I wasn't sure which one was Katie's brother, Josh. As soon as we reached the table, Katie started introductions. When she got to her brother, I could tell right away he was interested. I must have made a good first impression because it was clear he liked what he saw. His face seemed to light up when he looked at me. He went as far as to kiss the back of my hand when I reached out to shake his hand. I thought it was funny. It certainly loosened me up to relax and try to have a good time. We all had so much fun that night. We drank, we laughed, and we drank some more. It had been so long since I felt this alive and engaged; it was like I'd been a castaway rescued from a desert island. Most of the people at the table left around midnight, but Josh and I decided to stay. We left at closing and we left together. I spent the night at Josh's house. It was really the need for a human connection that drove me. I wanted to feel like a woman. I wanted to feel desired by a man. When you spend so much time alone, you begin to doubt your femininity and appeal as a woman. Our night together wasn't all fireworks or anything, but it wasn't terrible, either. The problem may have been Josh's small penis. I couldn't feel him inside me. It wasn't because I had a big vagina. He simply had a small penis! To his credit, he was great at oral sex—he could ignite a climax in me just by using his mouth and tongue. Because of that, I convinced myself that I could overlook his small penis. After all, I had to look at the big picture and consider my options. Josh was a potential husband, and a small penis or not, I had this fish on the hook.

As we spent more time together, other little alarm bells rang in my head. I began to notice that he exhibited some strong, effeminate, and definitely off-putting tendencies. I kept telling myself I could get past the little things I found unappealing because Josh seemed to be genuinely attracted to me, which made me happy. We instantly became a couple. Six months later, he relocated to my city saying he couldn't stand the thought of being away from me. This man *seemed* to adore me.

TRUTH BE TOLD | ALETHEA TAYLOR

My friends often told me they could tell how much Josh loved me just by the way he looked at me. I knew he did, but I didn't feel the same about him. I don't know if I expected the fireworks some people in love described, but maybe I wasn't used to the intensity of emotions love was supposed to represent. In my mind, I thought it was ok that my feelings weren't completely mutual. Perhaps one day my love for him would grow to be as strong as his love was for me.

But that day never came, and never would. **"Truth Be Told,"** now I see how dangerous my mindset was because it was driven by desperation and a sense that time was running out. I didn't want to miss what I perceived as the perfect opportunity to finally get what I wanted—a relationship. But a relationship is a living, breathing entity, not a brand of detergent you pick from a supermarket shelf.

Two years later, Josh proposed. I was so excited about getting married and the whole fantasy of marriage. My excitement about putting on that white dress was something I'd dreamed about since I was a little girl. I think I was just excited to be excited about all the glitz and glamor that came with a wedding. Deep in my heart, I wasn't in love. I was in love with the idea of marriage.

I didn't give any thought to any of the important details that came with marriage, like living with someone. Not dating. Not hanging out but living with someone full-time and seeing them every day, year after year. I didn't think about having to deal with his mood swings, his bodily functions, or his bullshit. I didn't consider the real face behind the masks we all wore when we met someone new. Everyone always looked and acted their best in a new relationship. Your hormones are in chaos and you acquire tunnel vision. But like a newly-minted coin, wear and tear eventually sets in.

I knew there'd be some good things, of course, but all the other stuff that comes with living with someone—the often unrealistic expectations we have of our husbands or wives never entered my mind. All I thought about was getting married. Josh was a good guy, so why not marry him? I wanted to start a family. At least, I thought I did until everything came into focus. Only then did I realize that my hunger to get married was as toxic as any other addiction. I craved it so badly I didn't care how I got my fix. And like most addicts, your habit eventually catches up with you.

After we married and had two children, things changed. I began to feel as if I'd lost me—who I was—what I wanted. I don't think I even recognized myself anymore even though my reflection in the mirror still looked like me. Everyone and everything was important but me. I'd always wanted children, but I never realized how hard being a mother would be, how demanding it would be, how much of me I'd have to surrender to ensure my children had everything they wanted and needed. In the process of taking care of them and making sure Josh was happy, I vanished. It was the same routine day after day. I felt like I was drifting through life in a fog like a programmed robot. We were just going through the motions like many other married couples I knew. Yes, we looked happy to outsiders, but to be truthful, *I was miserable.* Seems the grass wasn't greener on the other side after all. I just couldn't see past the fence.

People seem to believe that if couples are still together after several years that their marriages must be happy. That's such bullshit! We were seven years in, and I guess the old adage about the seven-year itch was true. Marriages are at their highest risk around the seven-year mark. It certainly was the case for us. I could no longer ignore my initial concerns that had been red flags for me when I thought about Josh all those years ago. His effeminate behavior became more annoying, and our sex life was never exciting. He insisted on sticking to the missionary position. He never wanted to try anything new, but I had a wild side that was constantly struggling to emerge. I was so happy to have a husband and finally enjoy sex the way I liked it, and who better to explore that with than Josh?

I never felt truly comfortable fully exploring my sexual fantasies with the men I had sex with. I didn't want to supply them with stories they could brag about to their friends. My fantasies were meant to share with my husband. I particularly enjoyed performing oral sex on a man, but it was never as fulfilling as I wanted because they always wore a condom. But having a man of my own whose dick I could freely suck without a condom was thrilling and something I looked forward to spontaneously doing. Unfortunately, Josh didn't seem to enjoy it. He did, however, take pleasure in performing oral sex on me. That was great, but I needed more. I needed some good penetration. Hell, I needed it dirty! To spice up our sex life, I tried introducing some sex toys and other things like role-playing, trying different sexual positions, and making love someplace other than the bedroom (the kitchen island sounded particularly erotic), but he was unwilling to try any of my suggestions.

The reality was that Josh was simply boring. He didn't appear to be very interested in sex at all while I had a high sex drive that he simply couldn't't satisfy. Couple that with the fact that love that was absent when we first got married and never blossomed as I expected, I was in constant turmoil! I had the marriage I finally wanted but not the level of joy I thought came with it. Half the time I didn't want to be around my husband, the other half of the time I was focused on the children. I felt like I had no outlet! Nevertheless, I still wanted the "marriage". I thought it was better to stay married regardless of how miserable I was rather than be single and lonely. Even when my frustration with my marriage approached a boiling point, particularly with our vanilla, non-existent sex life, I was still a faithful wife. I decided simply to deal with the choice I made until I discovered my husband's dirty little secret. He was fucking a stripper!

Once a month on a Friday night, Josh and a few of his buddies got together for a good ole "all boys card game". Supposedly, they sat around drinking bourbon, smoking cigars, and playing cards. However, I discovered that Josh and his friends were actually visiting strip clubs. The "all boys card game" wasn't a night of cards at all. Instead, it was a cover for my husband and his friends. I didn't know for quite some time that he wasn't going to his friend's house to play cards until I had an argument with one of his friend's "right now girlfriends".

Josh had a single friend who changed woman pretty often. It seemed there was a new one each month. Well, I got in an argument with a woman who was seeing his friend longer than a month and she had this entitled attitude as if everyone owed her something. We got into a disagreement over the phone one day when planning a couples' trip. Before I knew it, I called her a dumb bitch. She responded by telling me I was the dumb bitch because I didn't know my husband was fucking women at the strip club. So that's how I discovered my husband's dirty little secret.

TRUTH BE TOLD | ALETHEA TAYLOR

At first, I didn't believe her, but I conducted my own investigation and it was true. I was hurt, and to say I was angry was an understatement. Josh wouldn't make love to me, better yet, fuck me, because my level of sexual frustration demanded more than making love, it demanded a good hard fuck, which he wasn't providing. Yet, he was fucking a stripper. Really? I never led on to Josh that I knew. Instead, my anger led me to get even. I thought if he were doing it, this would be my opportunity to get the kind of sex I craved. One part of me resisted, but I felt he left me no choice. I didn't want a marriage full of cheating, nor did I want to be back out there fucking men who meant nothing to me, but I felt compelled to do it. It wasn't the life I wanted for myself. It was the excitement and comfort I needed to ease the hurt and isolation.

My job created plenty of opportunities to meet men. After contemplating my decision to pursue extramarital activities like Josh, I thought of my attractive co-worker who I knew wanted to fuck me badly. He even went as far as to tell me one day that if my husband ever messed up on me and he had the opportunity, he'd be more than happy to please me. He explained that he didn't want to fuck me, but he wanted to eat my ass and give me an ass-gasm. All he wanted me to let him do was to suck and lick my ass until I came. As appealing as his offer sounded, I always told him he'd never have such an opportunity to taste the menu, but after Josh's playtime with his strippers, I decided my co-worker was the perfect person to provide the sexual nastiness I needed.

For an entire week, I flirted with my co-worker to get him to respond. Just as I expected, he took the bait. He told me one day that I needed to stop looking at him so seductively or he'd wait until everyone left the office, throw me on the desk, and eat my ass. Bingo! Music to my horny ears! "When?" I asked. He was shocked into speechlessness, so he just laughed and walked away. I was disappointed but thought, *I'll tease him tomorrow.* When I saw him the next day, I said, "So I scared you?" He responded, "No, but I knew you were playing". I told him not at all, and if it were a game, to meet me in my office after work and I'd prove I wasn't playing. He nodded and walked away. I wasn't sure he was going to show, but I prepared myself for a good time.

When the day wrapped up and most people had left the office, I saw no sign of him. I waited around. Realizing I was the only person left in the office, I got ready to leave. I cleared my desk, stuffed my bag, and when I turned to unplug my laptop, suddenly, the lights to my office went out. I didn't know what was going on. I was scared at first until I heard my co-worker's voice. "So, you ready for me?" Still with the light off, and the excitement brewing like Vesuvius about to erupt, he approached me, grabbed me by the waist, and pulled me close to him. He kissed me roughly from my lips to my neck. Then he turned me around quickly and pushed me over the desk. I was so excited, so turned on, and so wet at the same time, I could have cum right then! I was wearing a dress but no panties because I wanted to be ready if he really followed through. He lifted my dress, stuck his hand in my pussy, and then told me to smell my scent before licking his fingers. What a fucking turn on! I was more aroused than I'd ever been in my life!

The next thing I knew, he was on his knees, ordering me to spread my legs and to stay bent over the desk. Just as he said, he started to lick my entire ass and instructed me to play with my pussy while he continued to lick my ass. OMG! Like an animal, he licked every part of my ass while I stroked my clit. I exploded within ten minutes. It was truly the best orgasm I'd ever experienced. Once I came, he got up off the floor, turned me around, and started to lick the juices gushing from my pussy. He rose, looked me in my face, and said, "Have a good night". What the fuck? My mind was completely blown! My legs felt like jelly. I collapsed into my office chair because I couldn't believe what had just happened. I was incredibly satisfied and felt more alive than I could remember. I just had to take a moment to collect myself. I planned to have only one encounter with my co-worker. However, that was just the beginning for me.

TRUTH BE TOLD | ALETHEA TAYLOR

The night with my co-worker was a fantasy come to life, but I knew it would be wrong to continue. I thought I could try one last time to persuade Josh to try something new and maybe enjoy the excitement I shared with my co-worker with my husband instead. So I set up a date night for us at a hotel in the city overlooking the water. I got there early and told Josh to stop at the front desk and get the key because I might be in the shower when he arrived and not hear the door. That wasn't true. I just wanted him to come and to see me all dressed up and ready for him.

When Josh arrived, he was excited to see me, and I immediately jumped on him. Of course, he started his predictable routine of eating my pussy instead of throwing me down and fucking me like I so desperately wanted. However, I had a surprise for him this time. As he started eating my pussy, I told him to eat my pussy from behind. This way, as he was licking my pussy, I could position my ass completely in his face. When he refused to lick me in that position, it killed any anticipation I had about the evening. All I could think was, *Here we go. Another boring night of vanilla sex!* It was at that point, and knowing his dirty little secret that I decided to continue to focus on me—to satisfy me! Josh left me no choice because he was unwilling to satisfy his WIFE!

Some of my long-married girlfriends were having relationships and sexual encounters outside their marriages. They told me all about them. I loved hearing the details of their sexual adventures and secretly envied the pleasures they got to experience. The liaison with my co-worker had unlocked the cravings I had suppressed most of my life. It was time to set myself free. I decided to join my girlfriends on some of their sexual escapades. It was the start of something thrilling, exciting, dangerous, and fulfilling for me! I'd heard about secret, underground sex clubs and swingers' clubs and things like that, but I'd never experienced them. Now, I was open to almost anything. I started hanging out with my girlfriends and visiting these clubs. My first experience at a sex club was pretty mild. All I did was watch people have sex, but one night I drank a little too much and got brave enough to engage. I explored every sexual fantasy I'd ever imagined, and I—was—hooked!

I started having casual affairs with men. We met during the day or early in the evening at my office or their workplaces to sneak in our sex dates. I had sex in parks, cars, hotel rooms, gyms. You name the place and I probably had sex there. Josh had no idea what I was doing outside our marriage. In his typical fashion, he hadn't noticed any changes in my behavior. He thought the difference in my routine was due to my new-found interest in exercising. I was going to SPIN classes, aerobic classes, taking yoga, and I joined a biking club. Josh was very encouraging, but he didn't know that most of the "activities" I told him about were cover-ups for my liaisons with various men. I did actually join a biking team because I was genuinely interested in biking events, but I also joined because I could meet men there—men who were more than willing to explore my sexual fantasies. It was an adrenaline rush beyond what I could have ever expected, and I was hungry for more. I thought I had the best of two worlds, I had the marriage I always wanted, and I was having unbelievable sex. I wish it would have been with Josh, but it didn't work out that way.

Before long, I found myself involved with a man who possessed wonderful qualities and was a sexual beast. I couldn't believe it! There was no way I could have both in a man. It simply didn't exist! But somehow, this man found his way to me. He knew I was married but still wanted to continue to see me. He thought he could handle the situation, but soon, he wanted more. He wanted me to be his, his woman, his wife. And as much as I didn't want to admit it, I wanted to be with him, too. Early in the affair, we'd both agreed that our relationship would be casual, but then we fell in love with each other. I was more torn than ever. Josh was a good man, but he wasn't the man for me. I wanted out my marriage, but for the sake of the kids, I had to stay. It was unfair to disrupt *their* lives because of my desires. I certainly owed them more than that. I didn't know what to do!

I was distracted at home and at work. Restless and conflicted. I had this great guy who satisfied me in more ways I could count. When I *was* with him, I didn't want to leave him. When I was home with Josh, all I thought about was being with my new love. I started to beat myself up, not because I felt guilty, but because I was living a double life and couldn't figure out a way to break free from my suffocating marriage. My distraction was becoming more apparent than ever. One night after dinner, Josh mentioned that I seemed very preoccupied lately. He asked what was going on. Before I knew it, I blurted out, "I've been seeing someone who I care about very much". I couldn't believe I said those words. I never wanted to hurt Josh, but I didn't want to lie to him anymore, either. He knew that our marriage was floundering, and I felt like I had nothing to lose at this point.

Josh just stared at me and a tear trickled down his face. He said, "I love you and I don't want to lose you. Can we work this out, please?" He got down on one knee, grabbed my hands, and asked if there was any hope for us. I felt terrible. Josh was a good man, a good provider, but we were miserable with each other. Oh, and let's not forget about his adventures at the strip club. The only difference was that he wasn't aware I knew about the strippers. I wanted to put everything on the table, so I told him I knew about the women he was fucking at the club. He seemed shaken and broke down. He admitted he was sexually involved with women in the club, but I wasn't quite right in my assumptions. I wanted to know why he didn't want to explore his sexual desires with me. He replied, "You're my wife, I don't feel comfortable engaging in dirty, nasty behavior with you." He told me that he held me in too high esteem to have me engage in the sexual activities he enjoyed. His reasoning made no sense to me, particularly because I was his wife and we should be free to pursue our sexuality however we wanted.

At that point, all the frustration and anger erupted from me with the violence of a geyser. I screamed, "I'm the person you should share those fantasies with! Maybe if we explored our sexual desires with each other, our relationship wouldn't be such a mess!"

Josh went on to tell me that he wanted to be dominated and penetrated by a woman, and he knew if he asked me to fulfill this fantasy, I'd no longer look at him the same. Once he shared his desires with me, it all made sense. While he admitted he wasn't gay, he enjoyed orgasms from anal penetration because it was the best climax he'd ever experienced. I couldn't help think that as much as I'd loved to engage in role play with my husband, fucking him wasn't the type of play I was interested in. I'm definitely open to exploring almost any sexual fantasy, but acting like a man while my husband acted like a woman didn't work for me.

The discovery of our secrets left us no choice but to dissolve our marriage and vow to work together to continue to build a loving, caring, and supportive environment for our children. He, like me, wanted so much more, but we both settled for being with someone for the one thing we wanted most in life—a family. Josh never felt that he settled, but you should be able to share your darkest secrets and innermost desires honestly and openly with your partner. He was never able to do that. Still, I can't place all the blame on him. I was guilty of marrying Josh out of desperation and putting my interests above anyone else's. I was selfish, and it wasn't fair to expect him to commit his life to a woman who wasn't completely in love with him. I learned the brutal lesson that making decisions out of desperation is never the right thing to do for yourself and your relationships. You find yourself in difficult situations that could have been simply avoided along with the pain, betrayal, and heartache they inevitably bring.

Truth Be Told, Josh was never "the one" for me, and I was never "the one" for him. Yes, we loved each other, but it was platonic love, or at least, platonic for me. We'd never been honest with ourselves or with each other. **Truth Be Told,** eventually, we were both thankful for our overwhelming misery because it pushed us to be our authentic selves and live our lives to the fullest. **Truth Be Told**, we owed each other the truth and should have shared it years ago. It was eye-opening to discover that while we were willing to share a life as husband and wife, we were never willing or comfortable sharing the truth about our true selves. **Truth Be Told**, we weren't living our truth, we were living a series of lies, and the sad truth was that we weren't living at all.

CHAPTER THREE

Hayden

He Cheated

*Every time he cheated, I took him back—the first time, the second time, the fifth time, the seventh time. Every time he cheated, I took him back in the name of love. Did I love **him** more than I loved myself? Why did I expect more from him when he showed me every time what he was about? Each time he cheated, I was more surprised than I'd been the last time he cheated, but why?*

We met years ago when he was twenty-two and I was twenty. We were so much in love. Devon was the finest thing I'd ever seen in my life. He was a nice guy, humble and quiet. He stayed to himself most of the time and all he did was work. I, on the other hand, was the more outgoing type. There was nothing shy about me. I liked being the center of attention. I was cute and had a body that made men look twice. But Devon was different. He *never* gave me a second look. We lived on the same street but when we ran into each other he just said hello and keep walking. It was different for me—*my* first thought was, "What's wrong with him?" He must be gay. He didn't swivel his head like an owl to look at me and didn't try to talk to me.

So one day, when I saw him coming home from work, I just stopped him and asked, "Are you gay?" He laughed at me, and said, "No, why would you ask me that?" Instead of waiting for me to answer his question, he shook his head and walked off laughing. I couldn't understand that. If he wasn't gay, how could he possibly continue to walk by me without trying to get my attention? Every other man did. From that point on, I knew I had to have him. He had to be mine! I didn't care if he had a girlfriend, a wife, or whatever, I just knew I had to have him. I planned how I'd go about getting him like a mission to Mars. After all, why not pursue something I wanted so badly? Other men couldn't resist me because of my bodacious booty. It was big, perfectly shaped, and I was quite proud of it. I remember my older cousin always told me, "Use what you have to get what you want". She also said that men always want some ass, so I was going to use mine to get him. I was going to use every weapon in my arsenal to make Devon mine!

The first step in my plan was to find out as much as possible about him. My best friend and I did a little investigating to find out where he hung out, who his friends were, etc. Luckily, a couple of guys we knew were friends with Devon. They all coached a little league basketball team at the local recreation center. We asked them as many questions about Devon as possible and discovered that he and his friends bowled every Friday at a place in the city. I wasn't a big fan of bowling, but I was going to learn to like it! We devised a plan to coincidentally show up at the bowling alley on the same night that Devon and his friends bowled. We planned everything down to the last detail. We knew the time we'd arrive, what I'd wear, the other friends we'd invite to make it look believable, and what I'd do to get his attention once we were there.

Three weeks later, it was time to execute our plan. We decided to arrive at 8 pm since the boys started bowling at 7 pm. I began getting ready for the night at around 5 pm. I wanted time to take a long bath and to prepare appropriately for the seduction. I selected a pair of my shortest shorts to showcase my booty, picked out the perfect crop top—one I knew would display my flat belly, abs, and just the right amount of cleavage, and carefully applied my makeup. Perfect! I looked like a model on the cover of a high-fashion magazine.

When we arrived at the bowling alley, I immediately scoped out the place. I wanted to find the open lane closest to the one Devon was using. Fortunately, we were able to get one two lanes away. There were five of us and we made sure we were noticed. We laughed and talked loudly and were extra energetic—anything to get his attention. We really did attempt to bowl and that was the funniest thing ever. Every time it was my turn to bowl I loudly announced, "Attention, the queen is about to bowl!" I made sure I bent down just enough so Devon and his friends could see my bootylicious butt peeking out of my shorts. I purposely rolled a gutter ball so I could ask him to show me what I was doing wrong. I wanted him to stand behind me and show me how to roll the ball correctly. Needless to say, by the end of the night, he was caught in my trap and agreed to come home with me. I told him that since we lived on the same block it just made sense. We were going the same direction anyway.

When we got to my house, we got right to it. I didn't want to waste any time. After all, I didn't want to give him a chance to change his mind. I put a spell on him and then took him on a ride he'd never forget! Sexually, Devon was everything I had imagined he'd be, and I was confident I was everything—and more—than he expected! We fucked all night long. My booty didn't let me down. I made sure the night was permanently engraved in his memory. I didn't ask him if he had a girlfriend until after our sexual encounter. Fine time to ask, I know, but it really didn't matter to me one way or another. In my head, if he had a girlfriend, I was going to push her out of the equation. As it turned out, he didn't have a girlfriend, but he did tell me he was dating. I wasn't worried about that because I was confident I could knock any woman he was seeing out the running for his affection. Years later, I'd come to regret the level of my conceit.

After that first night, we saw each other regularly. About five months later, I decided it was time for us to define our relationship, but Devon always blew me off and never gave me a straight answer. I kept bringing up the question and trying to force a response. I wanted to know if he considered me his girlfriend and if we were in a committed relationship. He actually seemed uncomfortable saying we were a "couple", or that I was his "girlfriend" but I badgered him until he finally said, "Yeah, you're my girlfriend." I think he just said it to make me happy and to eliminate the pressure I was putting on him to give me a title. Looking back, I don't believe he wanted to be in a relationship. If *he* had he would have asked *me* to be his woman, instead of me always saying I wanted him to be my man.

Truth Be Told, Devon didn't initiate our relationship. I chased him. He never sought me out. Either way, he said the words, and even if they were forced, that was good enough for me. Fast forward several years. By then we had a full-blown life together. However, as the years passed, I was still in "girlfriend" status and I wanted more. I continuously talked about taking our relationship to another level. I hinted about marriage but he never responded. I wanted this man to be my husband. After all, we were doing everything that married people did—we shared a house, we had kids together, we had a life together—we were a family. I pushed and pushed the issue, but Devon never even acknowledged the conversation, so eventually, I accepted the relationship for what it was and decided not to push the issue further. It didn't really matter much anyway because we always referred to each other as "my husband" or "my wife". The only thing missing was the "official paperwork" to back us up. Our lifestyle as a family was important to me and I didn't want to push him away. It had been hard enough to get this man to commit to the relationship and to agree to live together, so I just let the marriage thing go. I'd learned to pick my battles.

We were six years into the eleven years we spent together. I was pregnant with our third child when I learned about Devon's first affair. I'd gone to visit my mother and she and her girlfriend, Ms. Loretta, were sitting on her deck. Devon and I pulled up to the house in his car. He got out, opened my door, and helped me out the car. He kissed me goodbye, waved to my mother, jumped back into his car, and pulled away. As I walked toward the deck where my mother and Ms. Loretta sat, I saw them engaged in an intense conversation. Both women had surprised looks on their faces, and both were gesturing wildly—hands flailing about, feet stomping, and their eyes looked ready to bulge out of their heads.

When I reached the deck, the first thing Ms. Loretta said to me was, "I know that guy. We work together. Your mother said he was your boyfriend". My mother and Ms. Loretta hadn't been friends long. Ms. Loretta had just moved to the neighborhood a year earlier. Until that day, she'd never been around when Devon and I visited my mother. When Ms. Loretta said that she and Devon worked together, I smiled and said, "Wow, really? You work for the manufacturing company in the valley?" "Yes," she said, "I started working there five months ago around the holidays." Then she blurted out, "I was just telling your mother that he has a girlfriend who also works at the company".

I was shocked to hear her make such an accusation and told her that she must be mistaken. She said, "That's what your mother said but I know for certain that he has a girlfriend because we were all at the company Christmas party. I can show you the pictures." While Ms. Loretta fumbled through her phone looking for the pictures, my mother and I looked at each other shaking our heads in disbelief. I was in full denial because I was sure this woman was mistaken. There was no way Devon had a girlfriend! Ms. Loretta was also a scorned woman. Two years before, her husband ran off with her sister's best friend.

She came home from work one day to find her house cleaned out to the point where it looked like she moved. There was nothing left except the kitchen table and an old twin bed in one of the bedrooms. Though he left her clothes, he took two of her prized Chanel purses that he'd bought for her.

As a result, Ms. Loretta was bitter and vindictive toward everything and everybody—especially men. It was hardly a surprise that she wanted to prove Devon had a girlfriend. She was committed to exposing any man she thought was doing a woman wrong. In my case, she hadn't given any thought to my pregnancy or how receiving such information might impact me emotionally or affect my physical condition, especially if what she was accusing Devon of was true. Normally, my mother would have jumped in to stop this conversation, but this was something that could affect her child, her baby, and she didn't particularly like Devon. She always felt he was sneaky and couldn't be trusted. If he wasn't doing right by her daughter, she wanted to know about it.

Ms. Loretta finally located the pictures and handed my mother the phone so she could review them. My mother flipped through the pictures, all the time shaking her head. She finally passed the phone to me so I could take a look. Sure enough, there was a group shot of several people including Devon. He was standing between two women. Granted, there were others in the picture, but one of the women appeared to be slightly closer than she should have been. Devon had his arm around her waist, which I thought was unprofessional and inappropriate for a company event. Ms. Loretta was in the picture as well, so I knew they were all at the same company party. I felt the picture proved she knew Devon. However, it didn't prove he was having an affair and I told her as much. She said she could prove he was having a relationship with one of the women, so I challenged her to do it. She immediately dialed a number on her cell phone and put the call on speaker.

A woman answered immediately. Ms. Loretta started a casual conversation with her. She asked the woman how she was doing, how her kids were, and then she asked how things were going with Devon. The woman responded, "Devon, please, I'm not thinking about him". I sighed with relief because of the woman's response led me to believe nothing was going on, but then, she said, "He's mad at me because I wouldn't let him come over Friday. I told him I wanted to go out with my friends and it made him angry". She went on to say that while she was out with her friends, Devon was at her house waiting for her to come home. He called her repeatedly asking her to come home, but she was having too much fun. She said Devon felt she should drop whatever she was doing when he had free time because he desperately wanted to see her. In her opinion, he was just horny.

Suddenly, the ground started spinning and I lost my balance. My mother grabbed me and sat me in a chair. Tears streamed down my face. Ms. Loretta ended her call with the other woman once she saw how upset I was. It took some time for me to get myself together. Hearing that Devon—the father of my children, my soulmate, my partner, the man that I slept with every night—was having sex with someone he considered his girlfriend made me sick to my stomach, lightheaded, and dizzy.

Despite my reaction, I wanted to hear more and I begged Ms. Loretta to call the woman back. She didn't want to do it, but she reluctantly dialed again. When the woman answered, Ms. Loretta picked up their conversation where it had ended and asked her questions on my behalf. One of the questions was whether she knew Devon was expecting a baby. The woman answered, "Yes, I know he got a woman pregnant, but they're not together anymore". As the woman babbled on, Ms. Loretta covered the mouthpiece and quietly asked if she could tell her about me and let her know that Devon and I were very much together, but I begged her not to say anything. I wanted to handle this myself. I wanted to confront Devon with this, not deal with his alleged girlfriend.

TRUTH BE TOLD | ALETHEA TAYLOR

To say that I was shocked, confused, and hurt was putting it mildly. It felt like I'd been impaled by a twisting butcher knife. I spent the day with my mother and her friend as they consoled me and prayed with me and over me. I needed strength to go home and face Devon. Every time I tried to get up and move toward the door, my legs failed me. I didn't have the strength to face him while I was still processing his betrayal, so I decided to stay overnight with my mother so I could collect my thoughts. My mother phoned Devon to tell him that we'd had a wonderful visit that day and that I decided to stay the night because I was completely exhausted. I didn't get much rest that night, but it felt good to be at home in the comfort of my mother's arms.

The next day, I woke up with bloodshot, swollen eyes. It was clear I'd been crying most of the night. My mother prepared breakfast for me and helped me get myself together so I could return home to face the monster. That's exactly what Devon was to me at this point—a monster. I got home around one in the afternoon. When I walked in, Devon immediately noticed something was wrong. He thought maybe something was wrong with the baby, but I assured him the baby was fine. He was in the kitchen fixing lunch for the kids, so I didn't say anything right then. I didn't want our children to hear the conversation I had planned to have with their father. No matter how horrible I thought Devon was as a man, he was a great father and our kids adored him.

After lunch, we sent the kids to their rooms for naps. I still hadn't said a word to Devon. Before I sat down, I grabbed a post-it note pad and began to write. Devon sat down looking perplexed while he waited for me to finish writing. I wrote the name RACHEL on the pad, slammed the pad down on the table, and slid it toward him. As he read the name, I saw cold fear transform his face. I couldn't help myself. I started to cry. I couldn't hold back the tears any longer. As much as I wanted to scream and holler and curse his name, I couldn't speak. Can you imagine being so devastated that you can't speak? Well, that was the state I found myself in!

He didn't deny the affair with Rachel, but he assured me it was over. He said it happened, that it had been short, and that he regretted his actions and betrayal. He said that he was deeply sorry and promised that, if I forgave him, he would never betray me again. It was difficult for me to believe anything Devon promised. I couldn't think. The hurt I was feeling was too deep for me to decide about our future at that point. In the end, we broke up for four months until our child was born. I don't know if I was swept up in the emotions brought on by having our baby or by wanting my children to grow up in a family unit, but I managed to "forgive" Devon and we moved forward

together. It certainly wasn't an easy decision. I still
didn't trust him, but I loved him and ultimately decided
to stay with him despite his betrayal.

During the first year of our relationship, I
caught Devon out and about town with different
women. There were times when women texted me and
sent me pictures saying Devon was *their* man. I also
found pictures of naked women on his phone. Those
things were hurtful. We fought and broke up, but each
time, we got back together again. I knew he was dating
other women, but I considered them early relationship
casualties. I assumed he hadn't shaken all his old
girlfriends loose but I was convinced I was his main
woman. Back then, I could let the indiscretions go. I
didn't hold him accountable, but this time it was
different. We were in a committed relationship and had
kids. For some reason, I never imagined he'd cheat on
me.

Truth Be Told, I was having a tough time
forgetting Devon's affair. I told him I forgave him, but
in my heart I never did. **Truth Be Told**, in some ways,
I despised him. That manifested in how I treated him.
Whenever we got into an argument, I reminded him of
what he'd done and how badly he hurt me. I spoke to
him disrespectfully and did my best to tear him down. I
didn't hesitate to dog him out. Whether we were alone
or in a room full of people, I was seized by a rage that
erupted at unexpected times. When that happened, I

asked myself if I truly loved him anymore. I knew I didn't want to start another relationship and to go through the ordeal of getting to know someone new, so to keep moving forward, I convinced myself that he'd made a MISTAKE. I believed he'd never cheat again because he knew that if he did I'd take the kids and leave. That became my leverage, the weapon I could use to control him.

We moved on after that, but I don't know if things were ever really the same again. Two years after that affair, I had another baby despite the negative climate of our relationship. We now had four boys, and I knew that while I had his boys, Devon wasn't going anywhere. I also knew that I wasn't doing my part to keep our relationship alive. I was running on suppressed anger with the battle cry of, "I'm going to make him pay!" I wasn't behaving like his woman or doing my part to salvage the relationship. I acted as if everything and everyone was more important than he was. I actually found sleeping and eating more important than Devon. Because of my destructive attitude, I gained seventy-five pounds. Devon stayed active and trim. He was in the gym every day, playing soccer, or refereeing basketball games that required him to run up and down a court for hours. He stayed fit and healthy. He asked me to go to the gym to work out with him, but my idea of a workout was to pick up the phone to order food or to run to the refrigerator to grab a soda, some cake, or ice cream.

I knew I was letting myself go, but I had Devon's children and, after all, he owed me for cheating on me. I knew he wouldn't cheat again because I had the power to rip his heart out by separating him from his kids—and he knew it! That knowledge made it easy to justify denying him sex, never dressing up for him, and refusing to go out with him. I wouldn't caress him anymore, and no, I wasn't going to cook for him, support him, or love him. I spent most of my time with my family and friends and expected him to live like a monk—after all, he owed me! In spite of my behavior, my expectations for him in our relationship never changed. He was still fine as hell, but I had him by the balls. I had the kryptonite. I had his boys!

For a while, Devon continued to do what was expected of him. I started to regain my trust in him and believe he wasn't doing anything wrong and that he'd never dare screw around with another woman again. I settled comfortably into the relationship until the day he went out with his friends and came home drunk. I decided to check his phone. We had agreed, as a condition for staying together and learning to trust again, that we wouldn't lock our phones or add any special codes and we were free to randomly go through each other's phones. That night, I decided it was time to conduct a check. To my dismay, the stupid motherfucker forgot to delete his texts to another woman. Not only did he forget to delete them, but he also forgot to erase his voice messages. In the texts, he told her how much she turned him on and how he couldn't wait to see her that night, how he missed her and longed for her touch, and how he was going to lick her from head to toe! He was up to his old tricks again, pulling the same shit, messing around on me, and chasing booty! I felt so *stupid*. How could I have trusted him again? I asked myself why I continued to deal with his shit. If he didn't want to be with me, why didn't he just leave?

I tucked his phone in my pocket and waited for him to wake up and look for it. When he woke up the next morning, I was in the kitchen enjoying a cup of coffee when he came in searching for his phone. He opened cabinets and drawers and looked under chairs and cushions. I saw the panic beginning to set in. He finally asked, "Have you seen my phone?" I didn't answer, so he asked again, "Did you see my phone? My phone's missing. Damn! Where could it be?" I let him run around the house a little longer growing more frantic by the minute.

At last, he returned to the kitchen. He rubbed his head, looked at me, and asked, "Do you have my phone?" I reached into the pocket of my robe, took out the phone, and said, "This phone?" The fear on his face screamed, "I fucked up!" I shouted, "Sit before I throw this hot coffee on your ass!" I'd been pretending to drink coffee in an oversized cup but it was only very hot water that I planned to throw in his face if he lied. I asked, "How long have you been seeing Trina?" He immediately went on the defensive, jumped up, and started screaming at me, "You went through my phone!" I told him to calm his ass down and that he wasn't going to deflect shit onto me. This wasn't about what I'd done, but rather what he'd done. He tried to lie, but I don't know why he thought I'd believe him. I mean, the text and voice messages spoke for themselves. I'd already called Trina and had a conversation with her. She admitted everything, the dirty bitch! Devon and I got into a big argument and I threw the hot water at him. He ducked. The water got his arm but it missed his face. Too bad. I'd wanted to burn that pretty boy face of his, then he'd have seen how many women wanted him. I told him he'd cheated on me for the last time and to get the fuck out of my house.

For two years after Devon left, we just co-parented. I allowed him to pick up the boys, but he wasn't allowed to come into the house or spend time with them there. I always had my mother, one of my sisters, or a girlfriend hand the kids off to him and he dropped them off at one of their homes at the end of each visit. Not long into the second year, Devon got hurt on the job and I found myself running to his aid. It may be hard to understand, but as much as I wasn't interested in having a relationship with him, he was still the father of my children. I didn't want to see anything happen to him. I didn't need him but my boys needed their father. Devon spent a week in the hospital after the accident. He hurt his back, broke his leg, and injured a knee. I overlooked all of our past troubles and helped him through his recovery. I'm not sure how it happened, but during that time, things rekindled between us. I found myself deeply embroiled in our relationship again and before I knew it, baby number five was on the way.

Things went well for us after Devon's accident. It seemed like Devon had experienced a change of heart which helped him understand that what was important in his life was me and the boys. I thought, "Yes, I finally have my man back!" I was thankful for his new-found maturity. About three weeks before my thirty-second birthday, I started experiencing some issues with my eyesight. My vision was blurry at times, but I thought maybe it was due to allergies. I was having trouble seeing, but I dismissed the possible seriousness of my impaired vision until I shared my symptoms with my mother. She suggested I see my doctor. It was time for my annual visit anyway so the timing couldn't have been better. I saw the doctor immediately and shared my concerns about my eyes.

TRUTH BE TOLD | ALETHEA TAYLOR

She thought I should see an ophthalmologist and provided a referral for me at the Eye Institute.

A week later, I started cramping and bleeding badly. It scared me because my period wasn't due for another two weeks. I couldn't understand what might be causing this. The bleeding was so bad I soaked one pad after another. Scared out my mind, I called my mother and she rushed me to the hospital. While there, I was asked standard health-related questions, and one question was "Is there any chance you could be pregnant and possibly miscarrying?" The doctor asked if I'd been experiencing any other unusual physical issues, so I told her about my vision problems. Despite all the bleeding, the physician on duty performed a gynecological exam. Blood was drawn and sent to the lab and they gave me something to ease the pain. I was already worried and the look on my mother's face only made it worse. I was squeezing her hand so tightly I was afraid *she'd* have to see a doctor. I just couldn't fathom what was going on with me. I was so frightened!

Three hours later, the doctor returned to the room and said, "I'm sorry to tell you this, but you just had a miscarriage". I was shocked and asked, "What?" She went on to say, "The test and exam show that you were pregnant. You weren't far along". I just couldn't believe her words. Tears started streaming down my face. The doctor went on to add, "We believe the miscarriage and the issues you've been experiencing with your eyes were caused by the same thing. During the exam we checked for sexually transmitted diseases. Unfortunately, the test results confirm that you have chlamydia and gonorrhea." I couldn't believe what I heard. I was enraged, "WHAT? What the hell are you telling me?" The doctor explained that I had two sexually transmitted diseases. I heard her words, but they refused to register in my brain. I kept shaking my head and repeating, "What, what are you saying? What does this mean? How, how? Please explain!" She told me that some of the problems associated with venereal diseases are blindness, inflammation of the pelvis, and miscarriages if the disease isn't treated on time.

Due to the severity of my infection, I had to stay in the hospital for a few days. The doctor questioned me about my sexual partners and emphasized how important it was to notify each partner so they could get treatment. She also said that they should contact anyone they had sex with so they could also be checked. I was stunned. She was suggesting I had multiple sex partners. I was embarrassed that she assumed I was sleeping with multiple men. I wasn't sleeping around so I knew immediately who infected me. I was humiliated, enraged, astounded, and hurt. I was drowning in emotions from the loss of my baby, Devon's infidelity, and now I had to deal with two sexually transmitted diseases. What had I done to deserve this? I sobbed uncontrollably. All I could think was, "Lord, help me! Give me strength!" I was so devastated that I actually thought about killing Devon. He betrayed me yet again. He treated me like shit yet again, but more devastatingly, he played Russian Roulette with my life!

My mother was just as shocked and overwhelmed as me. Her child was in the hospital because of Devon's recklessness in having unprotected sex with women and endangering not only my life but our baby's. She wanted to hurt him, to return the pain he caused. Once she consoled me, she called Devon to let him know that I'd been admitted to the hospital. When he answered the phone, I heard her say, "Hayden is in the hospital and it's because of your no-good ass! You did this to my baby and I hate you for this! Quit playing with my baby's life. Just walk away, you no good, dirty bastard!" I heard him screaming, "What hospital, what hospital?" through the phone. My mother said, "I wouldn't tell your ass anything, but she wanted me to call you. As far as I'm concerned, you can drop off the face of the Earth!"

Reluctantly, she gave him the hospital information and he rushed over still clueless about why my mother was so enraged. When he arrived, I asked my mother to step out of the room. She hesitated long enough to give Devon the look of death before heading to the coffee machine. I turned to him and told him

TRUTH BE TOLD | ALETHEA TAYLOR

what was going on. My speech was fueled by the hatred festering in my heart. He gave me two sexually transmitted diseases that had cost us our child and ruined my health. My mind was in turmoil. I was trying to think of how I could get even for the way he devastated me. I wanted him to hurt as much as I did. I kept thinking, "He'd better prepare himself because I'm going to destroy him!"

The doctor came in during our conversation and explained the details of my situation. She asked Devon if he knew where he might have contracted the disease. She knew I hadn't slept with anyone but Devon. He was the source. Devon didn't reply right away, so she repeated the question. He hesitated and then finally said that he hadn't been sleeping around and speculated that maybe I contracted the diseases from sitting on a dirty toilet seat or possibly using a contaminated public toilet. The doctor shook her head at Devon's response and said emphatically, "No, these diseases can only be contracted through direct sexual contact." He didn't try to answer this time. Instead, he asked if she could also prescribe him some medication for the diseases. I finally exploded. "You motherfucker! Fuck giving you medicine, you nasty, no good motherfucker. I hope your dick falls off!" The doctor explained that it was important for Devon to tell us the truth and gave him all the reasons why. Finally, he admitted that he couldn't tell us where he contracted the diseases because he'd had multiple partners. I screamed at him again, "Go pack your shit and get out of my house!" Then I turned my back until he left the room. I was in the hospital for a couple of days, but those were among the worst days of my shattered life.

When I came home, my sister was there with my children. Devon was nowhere to be seen. To my disgust, I discovered he hadn't moved his things out of the house and was still living there. I grabbed a stack of his clothes and began tossing them out the windows, the doors, and down the stairs. I didn't care where they went. All I knew was that he had to go! Unfortunately, my children watched me throw out their father's belongings—his clothes, shoes, sneakers, jewelry, PlayStations, everything. I was yelling and screaming and talking to myself the entire time I tossed out his belongings.

My three older boys were watching me and screaming, "Mommy, Mommy, what's wrong? Where's Daddy?" I screamed back, "Your father isn't shit! He's a dirty bastard, a liar, a cheat. All he does is hurt Mommy, but not anymore!" The boys kept crying, "Mom, please stop, please stop!"

While I was in the middle of gathering Devon's things, he came home and tried to calm me down. We started tussling. The kids were terrified because they'd never seen us go at each other like that. When I realized how upset they were, I tried to calm down and pull myself together long enough to soothe the boys, get them a snack, and arrange for my sister to take them to the playground. With the kids out of the house, I returned to gathering Devon's things. He wanted to talk, but I didn't. Then I thought, "I need to find out who he's been fucking". I played nice for a minute and asked him calmly, "Who gave you these nasty-ass STDs?" He clutched his face, shook his head, and whispered, "I really don't know." "You don't know, or you just don't want to tell me?" I screeched. He said again, "I don't know." I slapped him hard on the side of the face and said, "Stop fucking lying to me! You know who you got this from and you better tell me before I hurt you!" He insisted that he didn't know and that he wasn't lying.

I didn't believe what he said could possibly be true. Of course, he had to know who gave him the diseases. I thought maybe he was trying to protect the bitch because I knew her. I started to get angry again, and I told him that he had one more chance to tell me who she was or there was going to be a big problem. I asked one more time, "Who gave you the diseases?" He replied calmly, "I don't know because I had sex with more than one person." "What? How many more?" My reaction was unexpected both to me and to him. I kicked him so hard that he flew out of his chair and landed across the room. He was really angry, but I continued to goad him. I dared him to get up and put a hand on me. He saw that I had a knife in my hand and I swore I was going to cut his ass. He got up off the floor and sat down in chair far away from me, but I walked over to him and got right in his face. I started screaming, "Who are they? Who are they?"

Devon finally admitted it could have been a girl he met at his friend's bachelor's party. He was drunk and paid a girl to give him a blow job, but then one thing led to another and before he knew it, they were fucking. He also admitted that he ran into the girl he fucked years ago who worked with him and Ms. Loretta. They shared an unexpected moment of déjà vu when they saw each other at the casino and he ended up fucking her in his car. Then there was a third girl—someone new—she was the cousin of his friend's girlfriend. They met during game night at his friend's house. She invited him to her place the next day and they fucked.

While he talked, I noticed some bottles of beer sitting on the kitchen counter that hadn't been put in the refrigerator. I reached for one of the bottles and busted that motherfucker over his head! He yelled and jumped up grabbing his head. He bolted out the house with blood dripping from his scalp. I didn't know where he was headed, and I didn't care, but I noticed he left his phone on the table. I took it and started looking through his messages and pictures. I was no longer surprised to see countless messages from women and pictures of women's breasts and vaginas, women masturbating, and messages he sent to one woman telling her that he loved her. I collapsed to the floor in tears because I couldn't believe this was happening to me, but the proof was right there on his phone. The worst of it was that he was in love with someone else.

I wanted Devon out of my life completely. He moved out and I moved forward with my plans to destroy him. He called and texted constantly, but I ignored all his attempts to connect. I kept him from seeing the boys and cut off all communication with them so he couldn't even talk to them. He wronged me for the last time, and now I was going to keep his boys away from him if it was the last thing I did. Our oldest son had a phone and Devon tried to reach the boys by calling his number, but I told the boys they were never to answer any calls or texts from their father. They couldn't understand why I didn't want them to talk to him. They missed him and cried and cried for him. I told the boys their father was a bad, bad, man, that he'd hurt Mommy, and couldn't be trusted. They still didn't understand and wanted to see and talk to their father. I was so angry with Devon that I told them if they talked to their father it meant they didn't love me. I went so far as to tell them that if they talked to him, I'd leave them. They cried. They didn't want me to leave them. They said, "Mommy, please don't leave us, please don't leave us!" I told them I would if they ever saw or talked to their father again, so they promised they wouldn't. I kept drilling it into their heads that Daddy was a bad man and that he'd hurt us. I told them he wanted to kill me and that they'd never see me again. They cried and told me that they didn't want Daddy to hurt me.

If I could just get inside their heads, I knew he wouldn't have a chance with them. I knew cutting his children off would wound him, and it worked. His mother called me at first begging me to let Devon see the boys. When I steadfastly refused, she told me how sorry he was. When that didn't work, she insisted that he had a *right* to see his children and not seeing his boys was killing him. I told his mother that he should have thought about his boys before he screwed around. I told her she could no longer see the kids and no one from his side of the family would ever be allowed to see or talk to them again. I made it my mission to turn the kids against him and warned them if they ever saw their father or if he tried to approach them, they were to scream and call 911 because he was going to try to take them away from me.

One day, Devon showed up at the kids' after school program. The boys saw him and started screaming, "He's going to kill us! Daddy's going to kill us! He tried to kill our mommy!" The program's staff called the police and he was arrested because I notified the school that Devon was trying to kill us and that I had a restraining order. That was a lie, but it was part of my plan to keep him from seeing the boys. I knew it would crush him! Whenever Devon called the house and one of the boys answered the phone, as soon as Devon said hello, the boys shouted, "We hate you! We hate you! You're mean! You're trying to kill Mommy!"

I kept the boys away from Devon for one and a half years before he finally got a judge to grant him visitation rights. At that time, I moved to Atlanta with the boys. That made it difficult for Devon to visit during his approved times. I successfully changed the image the boys had of their father. In their eyes, he was a bad man and they wanted nothing to do with him. There was once a time when they cherished their father and everything about him. They mimicked whatever they saw him doing and loved him more than anything. **Truth Be Told**, Devon was a horrible boyfriend, but he was a great father.

The boys had a rough time coping without their father in their lives. Admittedly, it was a huge adjustment. I never bothered to consider how tearing their father from their lives impacted the men they became. My only thought was to hurt Devon. The children weren't part of the plan. I'm ashamed to admit I used them as weapons in my war against their father. They were my kids and I was supposed to consider their welfare first, not use them as pawns in an emotional chess game. I know now that I had no right to do such a terrible thing no matter how hurt I was.

Truth Be Told, the children had nothing to do with the adult melodrama their parents were embroiled in, but in my anger, I hurt them as much as I hurt their father. I understand that I subjected them to catastrophic damage. They were too young to process, understand, or question my reasoning. **Truth Be Told,** I was the caretaker of their young minds and I used my anger to corrupt them with hate and bad memories of their father. My rage toward Devon blinded any rational thoughts. I learned the harsh lesson that children should never be used as pawns in any relationship. Deep down, I knew and believed the boys needed their father—that having a man in their lives was instrumental to their development as boys, young men, and eventually, adults. Even if we'd had girls, I knew that a father's influence is important to healthy development. **Truth Be Told,** I failed to separate my relationship with Devon from his relationship with his children. One had nothing to do with the other, particularly since they'd been shielded and protected from all their father's wrongdoings. It's a regret I live with every day.

Yes, Devon was a snake in the grass, a dirty, lowdown, good-for-nothing BOYFRIEND, but I couldn't tell you one thing he'd ever done wrong as a father. His kids always came first, and he did everything fathers were supposed to do for their children. **Truth Be Told**, he went above and beyond for his boys. Yes, he had some serious flaws when it came to our relationship, but they were characteristic of him as a boyfriend, not as a father. Some people may not understand or subscribe to my idea of the distinction between Devon the man and Devon the father, but there was a difference. I just chose to ignore it. I wanted to wound Devon as deeply as I was wounded, and I thought tearing his children away from him was the only way to make him feel my suffering even though it was our children who ultimately suffered the most. **Truth Be Told**, I couldn't in good conscience justify keeping the children from him. I was determined to distort their image of their father so I nurtured the hatred that eventually consumed them. I dug the knife of hurt into their innocent hearts. Their father wasn't to blame. I was!

Fast forward twenty years. The boys are now men, in relationships, and some have children of their own. They still didn't know the truth about what happened between me and their father. They still believed their father wanted to kill all of us. Looking back, I can't believe I nurtured that lie for over twenty years. It was finally time to come clean, if not for me, then for our children. It was New Year's Eve and I was thinking about what I wanted to change in the new year. I realized that before I could look to the future, I had to rectify how much I wronged Devon. That's when I finally decided to tell my children the truth about what really happened between me and their father. My conscience ached from guilt and what I had done weighed heavily on my heart and mind. It was time to confess my sins.

For a while, the boys were upset with me, hurt, and angry to discover everything they believed about their father was a lie. They now knew he never tried to kill me or that he never intended to hurt any of us. I asked them to forgive me and told them how deeply sorry I was but confessing my regret didn't change the reality of how differently they look at me now. They still love me, but I know instinctively they harbor contempt for me in their hearts because I disrupted their childhood. I lied to them about their father and kept them away from him during the most critical and impressionable years of their lives simply because I couldn't properly handle or process my hurt as a mature adult. My inability to deal with Devon and attempt to resolve our issues forever changed the relationship my children had with their father.

I continue to blame Devon for his selfishness, but **Truth Be Told**, I committed the most unforgivably selfish act of all by robbing my children of the opportunity to grow up with the man they loved so dearly—their father. As adults with the freedom to connect with their father, all are working to rebuild their relationships with Devon. It's my deepest regret that the damage can never be completely undone.

Truth Be Told, I failed to take responsibility for my selfish actions and decisions to stay with a man who repeatedly demonstrated his inability to commit to a relationship. I think the late poet, Maya Angelou, said it best, "When someone shows you who they are, believe them". No one forced me to continue the relationship. The only relationship that truly mattered was the relationship between Devon and his boys. I always had the power to leave and be true to myself, and above all, my children. **Truth Be Told**, Devon didn't play Russian Roulette with my life. I gambled foolishly with my own life and lost.

Truth Be Told, I wasn't only angry with Devon. I was also furious with the women Devon slept with because I felt they had no regard for me. It's quite ironic considering that had been my attitude early in my relationship with Devon. I didn't care about any of the women he was dating when we met. I was determined to win him like a carnival prize and was willing to do whatever it took—including eliminating any woman in his life—to claim him. I never imagined using my booty to snare him would also be the very thing I'd lose him to. I lived by the booty and our relationship died by the booty.

CHAPTER FOUR

Blair

The Other Woman

Dear Wife, I didn't set out to take your husband. I didn't set out to be the other woman. I didn't set out to be the side chick. I didn't set out to share a man. I didn't set out to get involved with him as more than a friend. No. that was never the plan. I didn't set out to purposely fall in love with him, but fate had other plans. Surprisingly, I found myself in a relationship with your husband. And despite what you believe, it just happened.

We met at a baseball game. He played on a team with a few of my friends. I attended the games frequently and after each game, large groups from both teams always went to the local bar for drinks, food, and celebration, which became our routine for nearly three months. Your husband and I talked often, as did everyone else in the bar. I never really gave our conversation much thought, I simply thought he was a nice guy. I noticed the ring on his finger, so I knew he was married, but I didn't think it had any bearing on our conversations. He always bought me drinks and food and checked on me while we were in the bar to see if I needed anything. I didn't find his behavior unusual because all the guys bought the women drinks.

However, on one particular evening, as I prepared to leave, your husband offered to walk me to my car. I said yes because it was dark and I was parked two blocks away. I welcomed the security he offered. When we got to my car, he hugged me and said it had been nice talking to me. I felt like I'd made a friend, a male friend, which was nice. He gave me his card and told me to call him if I ever needed anything. I looked at the card and saw that he was the district manager for a large auto repair/retail company. I also gave him my card and left. As far as I was concerned, that was it. A week later, the day before the next baseball game, I received a text message from your husband asking if I'd be at the game that night. I replied "Yes," and his response was, "I look forward to seeing you." Again, after the game, we hung out to eat and drink and, again, he made sure I didn't pay for anything. Not only did he take care of *me*, but he paid for my friends' food and drinks, too. At the time I thought, *What a gentleman!* I was impressed.

The night continued on a pleasant note. We laughed, danced, and just had a good time. He did tell me how attractive I was. He thought I was a beautiful woman with a great personality and he found me refreshing and attractive. At the end of the night, he walked me to my car again, hugged me, and told me to be careful. Before I got home, he called to tell me that he enjoyed my company and spending time with me and that he hoped to see me soon. He also told me that he noticed my headlight was out and that if I dropped by the auto shop, he'd replace it.

I called him the next afternoon to make an appointment to take my car into his shop. He told me there was no need for an appointment, just to bring in the car that day and he'd take care of everything. When I got to the shop, he was outside waiting to greet me and gave me a royal treatment. Not only did he replace the headlight, but his staff changed the oil because apparently, I never noticed it was overdue. I thought, *Damn, what a man!* He jumped right in and took charge, which I found immensely attractive. Some women may not have found what your husband did to be a big deal, but for me, it was, and I was impressed. To me, it wasn't a small gesture that he took care of my car. As a single woman, it was one less thing on my to-do-list to worry about. It felt good to have a man handle those kinds of tasks. When my car was ready, I thanked him and he responded, "I got you!"

Truth Be Told, once your husband said those words, I was intrigued because they struck a chord that stirred my deepest desires. I'd longed for a time when I could relinquish some of my burdens to a man I could count on who would genuinely and willingly help me.

After your husband took care of my car, I felt I could enjoy the benefits of such a "friendship" with him. To me, he was the type of man that any woman in his life could count on and could enjoy the experience of what it felt like to have a man tell you, "I got you".

While your husband did strike a chord with me, I was determined to have nothing more than a friendship with him. However, he began to call me more often to see if I needed anything or to see how my day had gone. It felt good to have a man check on me for a change. The phone calls quickly turned into lunch dates, sometimes, drinks, and then dinners. Again, I was of the mindset that your husband would only be a friend, but certainly a welcome presence in my life.

When we met for a meal or drinks, he always talked about his family. He spoke of you and the children with such love, I was astonished because I'd never heard a man express his love and feelings for his woman and family the way your husband spoke about all of you. He appeared to be a kind and caring man, and it showed through his actions, actions that not only intrigued me but stimulated a sexual appetite that had been dormant for some time. Still, I rejected those turbulent feelings and remained determined to be only friends. That is, until your husband surprisingly kissed me one night. Instead of pushing him away, I surrendered to his tender touch and kissed him in a way that transformed from friend to lover in a matter of minutes.

I clearly remember the moment your husband became "my man". It was the last game of the season and everyone was super excited particularly because the team had won the championship. Again, we ate, drank, laughed, and spent a night celebrating the big win. We stayed later than usual because the game was on a Friday night and no one had to get up the next morning for work, so we all drank a little too much. Your husband was feeling particularly happy after a few shots, which seemed to loosen him up because he was talking more than usual. He couldn't stop telling me how any man would be lucky to have me because I was a beautiful woman, and if he weren't married, he'd be with me in a heartbeat.

I laughed and attributed his comments to too many shots, but when it was time to walk me to my car, before I could get in, he grabbed my face and kissed me. I was surprised, but I didn't push him away. Instead, I gave in and enjoyed the kiss. I couldn't believe he'd kissed me. I couldn't believe what I was doing, but it felt so good! Eventually, I broke away, and when I did, he still held my face in his hands. He told me that I was beautiful and that he was sorry he kissed me, but that he also wasn't sorry he kissed me. He went on to say that he deeply cared about me, and I believed him because all his actions before the kiss proved that.

Of course, it didn't escape my mind that while he professed his feelings for me, he loved his family. I admired how he adored his children and how much he loved you. I know it sounds unbelievable to say that he loved you while he was in a relationship with me, but it was true. He shared with me how he took care of you, the things he did for your children, and he reminded me very much of how my father had taken care of our family. I always remembered how my father led our household and how loving, caring, and protective he was. He always took care of our family, but more importantly, he made sure that my mother never had to jump into his shoes. He always kept his promises, he did what he said he would, and we could always rely on him. He told me that a man wasn't anything if he wasn't a man of his word, so that's what I looked for in a man, and your husband always kept his word.

For a long time, I felt like I'd never truly savor the fullness of my womanhood while I was in a relationship because I'd never personally experienced, nor had I heard from any of my female friends, what it was like to be involved with a real man—someone who accepted his responsibilities as a man. Okay, I know that not everyone has the same definition of what makes a man a man, but I'd argue that if nothing else, a man should be the person that a woman could look to, turn to, and pull strength from. I never had any romantic relationships like that. I'd been too busy being both the man and woman because the men in my life weren't the type to step up and take their rightful places as men. I had to fill their shoes and mine.

With your husband, I discovered that I could simply be a woman. He understood his role as a man and proudly walked in his manhood. He didn't stroll, but rather stood strong and upright with a powerful, confident stride. I'd never been able to rely on a man to get things done, but when I called your husband, he kept his word. If he couldn't do it himself, he found someone who could. I could relax knowing that when he said he'd do something; it was as good as done. I never expected that an innocent conversation and an equally innocent offer of help would grow into something so special and, at the same time, so wrong.

Although I shared your husband without your knowledge, I didn't feel like "the other woman". I felt more like I was part of an unspoken polygamy pact when I knowingly began a relationship with your husband. I did so for my own selfish reasons, and once I was in it, I decided to enjoy it for what it was. Your husband had everything I wanted and he treated me like a queen. He provided everything I'd been missing in previous relationships and I relished that rare component he brought to our relationship. I knew we could never really be together, not only because he was married, but also because I didn't want a committed relationship.

TRUTH BE TOLD | ALETHEA TAYLOR

People so often believe that women who get
involved with married men are fooling themselves into
believing that they're entering a full-blown, one-on-one,
committed relationship, but that kind of thinking
shows a limited perspective. Not all women are out to
break up marriages or split up families. In my case, our
affair gave me everything I wanted *without* a
commitment, which was exactly what I needed at that
time in my life. I never tried to do anything to break up
your marriage. In fact, I did everything I could to help
him cover his tracks because I never wanted him to
hurt you or your family. There was no need to hurt you
because you didn't deserve to be hurt because of our
indiscretions. As careful as he was to make sure you
didn't discover our relationship, he never tried to hide
it and he never made me feel like I was a secret to be
ashamed of. We went out and about throughout the
city. We held hands, hugged, kissed, all in public. We
openly frequented local restaurants, took vacations
together, and he always made sure that we spent at least
part of special holidays together. He either came to see
me early in the day or dropped by late in the evening so
we could share some time together. He also made sure
we spent special occasions like birthdays together. All
of his friends knew about us. They loved me and cared
for me as part of his family. I'd been with single men
who were much more secretive about our relationship

than your husband. I never felt like a secret, even when I *was* a secret.

While we were both very clear that he'd never leave you and that I'd pursue a relationship when the right man came along, he didn't want me to consider another man. Contrary to widespread belief, women involved with married men aren't always the only ones to become emotionally attached. Men are just as likely to develop strong emotional ties as are women, and your husband developed those feelings for me. He didn't want me seeing other men. He insisted that he was my man—truly and fully. He gave me everything I wanted from a man, and I believe I gave him the main thing he was missing with you—excitement!

I took him to places he'd never visited. I had him try foods he'd never tasted, and sexually, he enjoyed experiences that until he met me, he could only imagine. Our sex life was incredible. The satisfaction we found in each other was something we'd both been missing. There were no inhibitions in our encounters, but please don't worry, we always used protection. I don't think he blamed you. After all, you married young and your lives together began with limited sexual experiences. He shared with me that he'd never enjoyed oral sex with you. He said it was something he desperately wanted to experience, but because of your strict upbringing, you didn't think oral sex was appropriate. Those things that you couldn't or wouldn't do, he was able to experience with me, which made him want to please me all the more. With you, he felt deprived of the excitement, the experience, and the joy of exploring a variety of sexual delights, but with me, he was able to experience all those pleasures, which we equally enjoyed.

I'm sure you're probably thinking that our affair was only about sex, but what we shared was an emotional, spiritual, and physical relationship. We often spent time together that never included sex. We simply took advantage of the simple joys and pleasures so many married couples often forget to do such as taking walks in the park holding hands, sitting by the river on a beautiful autumn evening watching the stars, or simply having a fun date night.

We did all those things and it sparked such happiness in us both. We truly enjoyed each other and cared deeply for one another. We became a family. Not only did we benefit from our relationship, but you did too. I know that the excitement and happiness he left with after being with me resulted in a stronger relationship with you. I truly believe I helped ignite the dying flames of your marriage. In some ways, we should be grateful to each other.

I admit I'm not proud that I had a relationship with your husband because I never believed in infidelity. I used to say I wouldn't think of getting involved with a married man, but sometimes fate has other plans for us, perhaps to teach us lessons. **Truth Be Told**, I realized through my time with your husband that life is complicated and precious. Not everything can be black and white, one way or another. Sometimes things just happen. They may be right or wrong, but what happens at that moment in time happens for a reason. **Truth Be Told**, your husband was what I needed at that moment in time, but I never pursued him. He pursued me and convinced me that we should be an "us", if only for a brief time in our lives. I know that I could have said no, but if it hadn't been me, it eventually would have been someone else. He needed to fill a void within his life.

I know that people reap what they sow, and when I finally unite with my special someone, the same situation may come back to haunt my relationship or marriage. I'm not sure what my reaction might be, but I'll be able to evaluate it through the lens of experience and with the perspective that, "Life happens".

Truth Be Told, we gave each other something that both of us were missing. Our time together was purposeful but, of course, bittersweet.

Signed,
The Other Woman

CHAPTER FIVE

Lauren

Unexpected Arms

I developed a hostile mindset toward men. I was tired. Tired of being tired and tired of being cheated on. I committed myself to men who professed to love me, who said they wanted to be in a monogamous relationship with me, but they all cheated. I was tired of good-for-nothing dogs cheating on me! I was tired of being hurt time and time again! I was just tired! I decided that I'd never again put myself in a position where another man could hurt me. That's how I found myself in the arms of a woman. Surely a woman would treat me better than any man would—or so I thought.

Every man I ever dated cheated on me. The cute ones, the ugly ones; I even got a fat man but he cheated on me too! It didn't matter what I did, how I treated them, or what I did to satisfy them. They all cheated! My past boyfriends had no regard for my feelings. It was always about them—their needs and wants, their selfishness and recklessness. They expected me to understand their behavior, their decisions, and their passive-aggressive reactions, and accept them as mistakes and issues they "had to work on". However, those "issues" kept occurring in our relationships more than I could count. There was no evidence of their attempts to do better or stop, only evidence of continued cheating and lack of commitment to the relationship. My last boyfriend, Fred, was so sloppy with his cheating, I don't even know how he thought he was getting away with it. But why should he worry about it? No matter how many times Fred cheated or mistreated me, I always forgave him and stayed. There were no consequences for his actions, no cause for remorse or guilt. So why wouldn't he continue? But there came a time when a knock on the door changed everything.

One day when my boyfriend and I were at the house we shared watching one of my ratchet shows, someone started banging on my front door like they were using a battering ram. When I answered, I saw a very distraught woman. At first, I thought maybe she had the wrong house, but then she asked for Fred. Before I could respond, she told me she was Fred's girlfriend and that he better come outside immediately. She looked pregnant, but I couldn't be sure if she was actually pregnant or just fat, but that wasn't my concern. I was busy thinking that she better calm down or I was going to call the police. How dare she come to my house demanding to speak to my boyfriend? If she knew he lived here, then she had to know he lived with me and that I was his woman! "What the hell are you doing coming to *my* house demanding to see my boyfriend?" I asked. She responded, "I've been trying to call Fred for two days and he's ignored my calls." "You're looking for Fred?" I asked dumbly. Frustrated, she screamed, "YES, YES, I'm looking for Fred!"

I asked her if she knew who I was, and she said that she did. She told me she knew I was Fred's girlfriend but that she and Fred had been seeing each other for more than a year and that she was four months pregnant and planning to keep the baby. She told me we'd better get ready because she was taking both of us to court for child support. I told the woman she could take Fred to court but she'd never get a dime from me because I wasn't his wife. This was the second baby Fred had with someone else since we'd been together. When I asked him about the pregnancies, he said they were accidents.

For the life of me, I couldn't understand how his dick continuously managed to "accidentally" slip into someone's pussy! I thought, *here we are again with another baby!* I felt like I'd been punched in my chest but the sensation lingered instead of dissipating. The longer the woman stood at the door demanding to talk to Fred, the deeper the pain. How was I supposed to deal with this? I accepted Fred's explanation about the first baby because it was conceived during one of our breakups. It still hurt, but I couldn't really hold it against him because we weren't together when the woman got pregnant. The most painful issue I had to face was that not one, but two women, would have biological children with Fred, but we didn't have any children. While I had a child from a previous relationship, I had none with Fred. I couldn't fathom how I'd deal with Fred and *his* children.

Three months before the knock on my door, I caught Fred with another woman who wasn't the one demanding to see Fred. I found out about her when I was driving down the highway with three friends. One of them suddenly started yelling, "Hey, isn't that Fred next to us? There's a woman in the car with him." I turned my head so fast I thought I'd get whiplash, but as soon as I turned to see if it was Fred, the driver moved to the far-right lane. My friend who was driving stepped on the gas and tried to follow. When I saw the driver, I realized it *was* Fred and there was a woman in the car with him. I told my friend to blow the horn and follow him. We were in the far-left lane, but my friend shot across two lanes of traffic to get behind Fred's car. I was hanging out of the window yelling, "Pull over! Pull over!" Everyone in the car was fired-up!

When Fred finally looked over, his expression was shocked and frightened. I told him to pull over again and saw how confused he was. There was an exit ahead, so I pointed, told him to get off, and pull over at the first street. We followed him off the exit. As soon as we stopped, I jumped out and raced to his car. When I got close enough to see their faces, Fred gunned his engine and pulled away, showering me with a cloud of gravel and dirt. He sped onto the onramp and took off down the highway.

I couldn't believe what had just happened! My friends, who had remained in the car, were stunned. They couldn't believe Fred could do such a thing to me. I was thoroughly embarrassed! Why would he take off instead of staying to explain himself and reassure me nothing was going on? I was mortified and furious! My friends didn't think we should follow him anymore. They said it would be too dangerous because we'd have to drive too fast to catch him. I wanted to go after him and ram him like a bumper car!

My night was ruined, but my friends persuaded me not to let him spoil my evening. That, of course, was easier said than done. There was no way I could sit quietly in a dark movie theatre, so my friends suggested we change our plans and head to the nearest bar for drinks. We found a bar nearby that had great music and there were plenty of men offering to buy us drinks. The place was just lively enough to take my mind off Fred's behavior.

About three hours later, I decided to go home. When I opened my front door, I found Fred sitting on the sofa as if nothing had happened. He had the audacity to come home and sit and relax until I returned. I thought, *Seriously?* Of course, he gave me some bullshit story about how he was giving a friend a ride and that he sped off because he didn't want me and my friends to hurt her. He was more worried about the woman than about how I felt! I didn't believe him, of course, but I didn't leave him either.

The day the woman came to my door demanding to see Fred was when I finally had enough. It gave me the courage to leave him. I wondered how many women he actually had. He couldn't possibly love me or want a committed relationship if he kept having affairs with all these women. It was just too much for me. At that moment, with that woman yelling in my face, my faith in men was completely shattered. I blocked out her voice and considered how Fred was having sex without condoms and then coming home to have sex with me and exposing me to all sorts of diseases.

It took me back to my relationship with my previous boyfriend, Ethan, and what I endured in that relationship. Ethan and I had been living together for 1½ years when I discovered that instead of paying the bills from our joint bank account, he was taking money for his own use. By the time I discovered what he was doing, he had stolen over ten-thousand dollars. When we decided to move in together, we thought it would be a good idea to get join accounts so we could equally pay the bills each month. A portion of my bi-weekly paycheck went to our joint account and the other half to my personal account. Ethan oversaw paying the bills and I trusted him to do so.

I remember one day heading to a meeting at work and getting a call from my car finance company asking me if I planned to bring my account current before they repossessed my car. I immediately assumed the call was a mistake because my car payment had always been on time. I knew Ethan was paying the bills because I never saw any notices in the mail about late payments. Well, the caller went on to inform me that it was indeed my account and verified the information. I was completely dumbstruck. I couldn't believe Ethan hadn't made the car payment and couldn't imagine what he did with the money.

I was furious! I thought, *what the fuck was going on!* I didn't call Ethan after my conversation with the finance company because I didn't want him to know I knew about the missed payments. I wanted to uncover all the information I needed before confronting him. After I hung up, I continued to my meeting, but I was completely distracted. I was supposed to make a presentation to a group of clients but I didn't think I'd be collected enough to manage it.

Unfortunately, I had to make up an excuse that I was ill and couldn't do the presentation. Thankfully, a colleague was able to step in. In reality, it wasn't a lie. I felt sick to my stomach. My car was about to be repossessed, not because I didn't have the money to make the payments, but because they were missed. I had to find out why. I parked out of sight worried that if my car was scheduled for repossession, my house and workplace were the first places the finance company would look for it.

As I sat in my car, I called my car insurance company, the utility companies, my credit card company, and the bank where we had our joint checking account. To my surprise and disgust, Ethan hadn't paid either of our car payments, our car insurance had lapsed, and he racked up ten-thousand-dollars of charges on the credit card. I was devastated. I checked the credit card statement to discover that he charged shoes, clothes, and jewelry for himself, but more shockingly, I discovered there were charges for women's purses, shoes, and clothing. I even saw dates to spas and hair salons. Once I saw the charges for women's shops and salons and the spa visits, I called our cell phone company to get detailed copies of phone activity for two months, which included the dates of the credit card charges.

I noticed Ethan called one particular number every day, several times a day, and specifically during days when the credit card statement showed charges for the spa. I decided to call the number. As I expected, a woman answered. I told her who I was and that I was calling because I discovered from Ethan's phone log that he called this number quite often. She didn't hesitate. She told me that she and Ethan had been in a relationship for a few months, but she had no idea he had a girlfriend. She told me he spent all the money on her and her children and that he'd even bought her teenage son a used car. I couldn't believe what I heard. Ethan was using my money on another woman and her family and not paying my bills.

When I finally got home, Ethan already knew what happened because the woman called him. When I saw him, "I asked him why, why would you do such a thing to me, why? I thought you loved me. Why would you do this? Why would you take my money?" He looked me in the face and said, "I don't want to hurt you!" But I told him he'd already hurt me by lying and stealing from me, and that I deserved the truth. He said he cared about me, but he wasn't in love with me. He'd felt this way for some time but didn't know how to tell me. He stayed because he enjoyed the lifestyle we could afford together. But what he was really enjoying was what my money and credit cards allowed him to do. He said he intended to repay me, but greed got the best of him. Before he knew it, the situation was out of control. I accused him of not only spending my money but being in another relationship behind my back. He admitted that he loved the other woman and was planning on leaving me to be with her.

I'll never forget the grief and agony that overwhelmed me. My body was on autopilot. To hear that someone I loved was with me only because of what I could give him and not because of any genuine feeling was heartbreaking enough. But to hear that he was in love with another woman was the ultimate betrayal. I could barely see from the rushing tears in my eyes.

Ethan left that night. I couldn't believe he was capable of hurting me in such a callous way. So when the woman knocked on my door looking for Fred, that horrible experience with Ethan resurfaced. I'd become yet another casualty of a man's selfish behavior. Combined with my crumbling relationship with Fred, I completely lost all faith in men and their capacity to maintain loving, faithful relationships.

Two days after the encounter with the woman at the front door, I packed my bags and left Fred. I took my son and moved in with my cousin, Kellyanne. Kellyanne was my favorite cousin. We were like sisters. She was the first person I told about the woman at my doorstep and she immediately offered her house because she knew I wanted to get away from Fred. I was thankful for her support and help as I was so distraught, all I did was cry and hide in my room. She took care of my son and took him out as much as possible because neither one of us wanted him to see me in my sorry state. I needed some time alone and she made it possible by stepping into the role of mommy for a little while.

While Kellyanne gave me space to process my situation and deal with my feelings, she wouldn't allow me to sulk for long. She told some of her friends what I was going through and they were also incredibly supportive. She had a wonderful group of friends. These women were always helping each other through situations and they offered the same support to me. They rallied around me when I needed them most. When we got together, there was certainly some man-bashing, but for the most part, it was simply good women helping another woman through a rough patch. They really didn't mind joining in when I talked smack about men because they had no interest in men. All of my cousin's friends were lesbians and couldn't have cared less when I began ranting. Some of them told some mean but funny jokes about men that kept me laughing through a dark period of my life and helped with my healing process.

One evening, my cousin and her friends were going out for a night on the town. They met at my cousin's house for a few drinks before heading out. They asked me to join them, but I didn't feel like going out. I wanted to stay in the house and have a pity party. Besides, I'd never been to a gay club and wouldn't have known what to expect or how to behave. I watched my cousin and her friends prepare for their night out. They started with some drinks, then they put on some music and started dancing and getting hyped. Suddenly I thought, *Why shouldn't I go out and have a good time with them?* I didn't have my son that night. He was staying with my mom for the weekend. I decided I needed to have some fun. It was Saturday night. Why would I want to sit home alone? Decision made, I jumped right into the festivities. I had a couple of quick drinks before we left so I could catch up with the others, and then we were off.

We partied our way through several bars around the city. The gay club was our last stop. By the time we got there, I was no longer nervous. After several drinks, I felt good. Now I wanted to DANCE. The club was nice and was one of the best clubs I ever visited. When we arrived, we headed straight to the dance floor because the music was amazing! I think we danced for fifteen minutes straight. After all that dancing, we needed to find some seats and get some drinks. I managed to find a seat at the bar and ordered a round for everyone. Three of us were drinking and talking when the mixologist interrupted and told me he had a drink for me. I hadn't ordered another drink and told him so. He gestured toward someone at the other end of the bar and told me the drink was on her. I looked where he pointed but all I saw was a man. I thanked the mixologist for the drink and continued to enjoy myself.

Soon, I received another drink, and then another. I accepted all of them and by the third drink, the person who bought them decided to come over to talk to me. As he approached, I thought, "Wow, he's dressed nice and looks good." I began to pick up hints of his cologne. *Oh, he smells good too,* I thought. I said hello, and only when he responded did I realize that *he* was a woman; Carol. I completely forgot we were in a gay club. I greeted her pleasantly and thanked her for the drinks. We began talking and quickly became engrossed in conversation. I told her what I was dealing with and she shared that she'd recently been engaged to a man. They were planning a big wedding when she found out he had a wife and child living in another state. After that, she stopped dating men and started dating women. She said she'd always been attracted to women, something I never felt, so she decided to explore relationships with women. I told her my preference was men but that I didn't know if I could ever trust another man again. Have sex with them, yes, but I was unsure if I could deal with a relationship.

Talking to her, I didn't feel like I was with a woman. Perhaps it was the way she was dressed along with all the drinks that changed my perception. She kept calling me "babe", all her mannerisms were masculine, and the more we talked, the more I forgot she was a woman. When a great song came on, she grabbed my hand and led me to the dance floor. I thought nothing of it because I was used to dancing in a circle with my friends when we went out, so dancing with a woman was no big deal. I felt good after all the drinks, the music was jumping, so when we started to dance, she pulled me close and started touching me. It was nothing alarming because I've danced close to my friends and we've touched each other's asses. When the woman touched me, I had to admit it felt good. She kept telling me to "Get it, baby. Do that thing. Work that body!". Then she told me how good I looked, and the more compliments she gave me, the more I worked my body and let loose.

The next thing I knew, she turned me around to face her and leaned in for a kiss. At first, I hesitated, but then I kissed her back. I was surprised that I kissed her, particularly because I never had any interest in a woman. It was a quick kiss and she apologized immediately, but there was nothing to apologize for. I was teasing her, and I think I wanted her to kiss me to see what it would be like. While it was no different from kissing a man, I wasn't completely comfortable with it either. She wanted me and it felt so good to feel wanted and desired I just relaxed and let it happen. My cousin and her friends were astonished as they looked on laughing, but they didn't interrupt me. They just watched from a distance and let me enjoy the evening because they knew it was what I needed.

After that night, I started hanging out with Carol as strictly friends. She was a nice, compassionate, understanding woman. I felt a real connection with her, particularly because we had similar experiences with cheating men. I felt she understood my pain and struggle more than anyone else could. Admittedly, I was also using Carol. I knew she had romantic feelings for me. She catered to my every need and I enjoyed the attention. She made sure I had whatever I or my son needed. I knew she did this because she wanted me, but I just needed to feel wanted.

One day, when I returned from a night out with Carol and some of her friends, Kellyanne asked if we could talk. She seemed tense and on edge. I assumed she was still upset because she and her girlfriend had a big blow up a couple of days earlier. She began by telling me that she noticed how much time I was spending with Carol and it concerned her. I was shocked. Carol and I were friends. Why would Kellyanne be concerned about that? When I asked, Kellyanne said she believed I was leading Carol on and that I was wrong to do so. I became defensive and asked why she thought I was leading Carol on? I wasn't prepared for Kellyanne's aggressive response. She accused me of being full of shit and that I was acting like a man. Now I was really confused. Kellyanne said I shouldn't get involved with Carol unless I wanted to be in a relationship with her. I told Kellyanne that I loved men, but after spending a lot of time with her and her friends, I became curious about a relationship with a woman, particularly after observing how Kellyanne interacted with her girlfriend. Kellyanne angrily replied that she was sick of straight women turning to gay women when a man hurt them simply to use them for comfort, and then leave them once they healed enough to move on. She said it was fucked up to use Carol the way the men in my life had used me.

Kellyanne went on to tell me she was a gay woman. It was who she was and had always been. In a brutally honest moment, she told me she didn't believe I was gay, nor had a desire to be with a woman, and that I was using my disenchantment with men as an excuse to get what I needed from Carol with no intention of committing to a real relationship. I didn't respond, but we both knew she was right. Like a junkie, I craved the attention Carol gave me. It made me feel desired, cherished, and I needed it to climb out of my slump. Kellyanne gave me an ultimatum. Get my shit together and stop playing with people. It wasn't right. I really didn't care what my cousin had to say, I was going to do what I wanted to do.

About a month after my conversation with Kellyanne, Carol and I were hanging out at her place drinking and watching a movie when she suddenly turned to me, gently grabbed my face, and said, "I really care about you and I want to make love to you."

I knew she cared about me, but I wasn't expecting her to tell me she wanted to make love to me. I looked in her eyes and clearly saw the feelings she had for me. The expression on her face touched my heart and I instinctively started to kiss her. One thing led to another and soon we were making love. But to be technical, she was making love to me. She didn't want me to please her in any way. She wanted the sex to be all about me. Knowing that I'd never been with a woman, she wanted to show me what it was all about. At first, it didn't feel natural to me. I hesitated as she began to touch me, but after everything she'd done for me, I felt a sense of obligation, as if I owed her my body. To get through the experience without disappointing Carol, I closed my eyes and pretended she was a man.

Once I closed my eyes, I couldn't tell the difference. She was incredibly gentle. She caressed me and took her time exploring my entire body, which was something no man had ever done. I didn't have to tell her what to do to please me or to move into a certain position to receive more pleasure. When she performed oral sex on me, she softly licked every inch of me. It was unbelievable. When I orgasmed, it was like nothing I'd ever experienced before. In fact, I squirted all over her face, but she enjoyed it as much as I enjoyed climaxing. The adage that a woman knows how to satisfy another woman better than a man was certainly true. No man I'd ever been with made me explode the way Carol did.

After it was over, I didn't know how to act, what to say, or where we were headed. She knew I was confused and reassured me that we didn't have to have sex again if I didn't want to and we didn't have to put a label on our "friendship". I was happy to hear her say that because I needed some time to digest the experience. I didn't see Carol for a week because I didn't feel as confident or comfortable with our friendship anymore. As I've always known, sex changes everything between two people and it certainly changed and complicated things between us. Yes, I enjoyed the sex, but it still didn't feel completely natural to me, and I couldn't change my mindset no matter how tight I closed my eyes.

I knew I'd eventually have to talk to Carol about my feelings, but out of a selfish fear of losing her attention, I acted as nothing happened between us. We continued our friendship, and I allowed her to occasionally make me cum. Just when I thought I was in control, I started to develop feelings for Carol and a year later, we were in a relationship and living together. It was surreal, but I was in a relationship with a woman. Carol was good to me. She was more emotionally supportive than a man and I appreciated that support. Our "love life" was one-sided but to my surprise, Carol didn't mind, although I didn't understand how. She always satisfied me physically, but even though I didn't reciprocate, she told me my satisfaction was enough for her.

Everything was great until the day we got into a heated argument. We'd been hanging out with some friends and I casually mentioned how pretty I thought one of the women was. Carol assumed that meant I was interested in the woman. I told her I wasn't interested and was just making an observation, but she thought I was being disrespectful by making such a statement. It was nothing more than an innocent comment. I tried to explain that to her, but she wasn't having it. She gripped my arms and pushed me against the wall. She told me I'd better not even think about being with someone else because I belonged to her! For the first time in our relationship, I was frightened. I couldn't believe she physically put her hands on me, threatened me, and overreacted to such an extent. Alarmed by her behavior, I pushed her away and ran away crying.

Later, she apologized several times and promised never to put her hands on me again. I believed her. I accepted her apology and we moved on. We were in love and in a good place until she exploded again. It was New Year's Eve and we'd invited about fifteen people over for the evening. While we were drinking, singing, and playing games, I spilled a drink on myself and went to the bedroom to change my stained clothes. When I returned to the party, I was wearing shorts and a half-shirt. I'd just walked into the kitchen to make some fresh drinks when Carol came over and started yelling at me. "What the fuck do you have on?" she screeched. I looked at her in shock. "What are you talking about?" I asked. She grabbed my arm and started to pull me into another room, but I dug my heels in and wouldn't go. My friends quickly came to my rescue and told Carol to let me go. Someone asked her what was going on and she replied, "She's dressed inappropriately. I want her to go put some clothes on right now!" I told her I wasn't going to change and to "deal with it". Before I knew it, she slapped me and we broke into a full-blown fight. Our friends tried to intervene and stop the fight, but we weren't listening.

It was ugly. I grabbed several bottles and threw them at Carol because she punched me with her fists. The others stood awkwardly on the sidelines. Exhausted, Carol and I finally separated. I grabbed a few things and went home with two of my friends. I stayed with them the entire weekend. Carol called constantly begging me to come home. She tried to excuse her behavior by saying she'd had too much to drink. I didn't buy it. I was clearly reminded of her bad behavior every time I looked in my mirror and saw my huge black eye. It didn't occur to me that I was a battered woman in the middle of a domestic violence situation.

I stayed with my friends for an additional week. Carol sent flowers, cards, text messages, and wouldn't stop asking me to forgive her. She even sent proof that she registered for an anger management program. She definitely pulled out all the stops. Again, I accepted her apology. We resumed our relationship and I moved back into the house. Months passed and we were doing well. The anger management classes seemed to help, but then Carol decided I was spending too much time with one of my co-workers. Each year, my company hosted a retreat where employees from all four company locations got together for a couple of days. It was an opportunity to interact face-to-face with co-workers from around the country. It was good to meet people I worked closely with via phone and email but seldom saw in person. I worked with one woman, MaryAnn, for six years and we became good friends during that time. We agreed to share a room at the retreat as we had several times in the past.

One evening, after Carol and I finished dinner, I mentioned that MaryAnn and I would be sharing a room at the retreat. She responded by saying, "You're going to share a room with that bitch, MaryAnn?" I was surprised that she called MaryAnn a bitch. She was a good friend of mine. Carol knew MaryAnn. She'd been a guest in our house on several occasions. Carol had always, in some small way, seemed to be jealous of MaryAnn and our friendship. She said things like, "MaryAnn likes you. She wants you. If you gave her half a chance, she'd sleep with you." Carol wouldn't listen when I told her she was completely wrong. I said, "MaryAnn is in no way interested in women." But Carol replied, "Neither were you until I came along." I laughed it off and shook my head. Carol became extremely jealous and insecure even though she had no reason to feel that way. I always told her how much I loved her and that I wasn't interested in anyone else. I was perfectly happy with our relationship.

A week before the company trip, I was picking out my wardrobe when Carol came into the bedroom and started grilling me. I explained again about the conference and what was going to happen there. She seemed fine until I got to the part about sharing a room with MaryAnn. Once again, she flipped. She insisted I couldn't share a room with MaryAnn and told me that unless I changed my room, I couldn't go. I laughed at her, turned my back, and continued pulling out clothes to pack. Carol gave me a hard shove and I found myself sprawled on the floor. She jumped on me, started slapping me, and told me I wasn't going to ignore her.

We began to fight in earnest. I was crying hysterically as I tried to defend myself. Once again, I couldn't believe this was happening to me. I managed to get up from the floor and headed for the front room to get my purse and car keys, but before I reached the door, Carol grabbed the car and house keys and wouldn't return them to me. Her anger management training didn't seem to help as she began yelling and knocking things off the shelves.

Before I knew it, she picked up the phone and started dialing. When the person on the other line answered, she shouted, "Bitch! You better stay away from my girl!" I screamed, "Who are you talking to?" She replied, "MaryAnn." I was beyond humiliated and embarrassed. I tried to grab the phone from Carol and hang up, but when I got close, she pushed me so hard that I fell onto the glass table. I cracked the top and banged my hip on the edge of the table as I fell. Carol didn't bother to help me but finally hung up the phone. Instead of asking if I was all right, she told me she was seeing someone else. She said she was done with me and then stormed out of the house, took my car, and didn't return for two days. She seemed surprised to see me there when she got back, but I wanted a chance to tell her what I thought of her.

I told Carol that my relationship with her was worse than any relationship I had with a man. I explained that none of my ex-boyfriends had ever put their hands on me, hit or abused me, yet I allowed her to mistreat me so I could no longer stay in the relationship. She tried to justify, apologize, and promise it would never happen again, but I knew it was impossible for her to make, let alone keep, such a promise considering our history. I knew I couldn't stay with someone who mistreated me. I left and never looked back.

Truth Be Told, after my breakup with Carol, I spent some time alone to take a step back and determine why I continued to find myself in such destructive relationships. I finally realized that I constantly rushed into relationship after relationship. Ethan and I moved in together after knowing each other for only three months. Fred and I moved in together after six months, and Carol and I after one year. My shortcoming was that I never allowed myself time to get to know someone. It was almost as though I was racing against the clock in the fear that if I didn't move in with someone, I risked losing that person.

But relationships aren't a race. I learned the hard and painful way that rushing isn't the answer. The lesson for me was to move forward slowly and cautiously because it's critically important to know who a person truly is. I know there's no specific "timeframe" in getting to know someone that guarantees they won't turn out to be completely different from what you thought or expected. However, dating someone for a period of time allows you the opportunity to learn more about them and who they are.

TRUTH BE TOLD | ALETHEA TAYLOR

Truth Be Told, I thought being in a relationship with a woman would be better than being in a relationship with a man. I thought it would protect me from cheating, but it never crossed my mind that women also cheated. I understand why she cheated. I'm not saying it was right, but I understood. I wasn't willing to satisfy her sexually, so she sought that elsewhere. I selfishly wanted all the perks of a relationship without the commitment of a partner. Nevertheless, I believe that instead of cheating, we could have simply gone our separate ways.

Truth Be Told, I never imagined a woman would subject me to both mental and physical abuse, but Carol did. I didn't know that women subjected each other to the same pain and heartache as men. Carol had no right to physically abuse me because she was a woman. Abuse is abuse. It's unacceptable in any situation! **Truth Be Told,** it's important to be with someone because you want to be with that person wholeheartedly. I never felt completely at ease with Carol. When you start a relationship with someone, it should be with the commitment to truly meet the needs and desires of that person. **Truth Be Told,** I desire a man, and after my experience with Carol, I no longer believe that men treat women worse than women treat each other. I have learned that relationships are a gamble regardless of gender because we all share the same human qualities. A person's gender doesn't determine how he or she will treat someone. That has to come from the heart.

CHAPTER SIX
Royce
Potential

I fell in love with a man that I should have never considered as a mate, but for some reason, I was drawn to his "potential".

I was raised by my parents to always do my best and expect the best—do better to be better. They told me to go to school and get good grades so that eventually I could get an excellent job and afford to live an affluent life. I was raised to believe that I could do and be anything I wanted, and I believed it. I was taught to give my best because you only get out of it what you're willing to put into it. If I wanted a good life, then I had to work hard to obtain it. The finer things in life required meeting a specific set of expectations. I lived by those expectations. I set goals for myself and was able to create a life that I could be proud of.

I had it going on—I was well-educated, I was the top engineer in my firm, I drove a Range Rover, I lived in a $400k condo overlooking the water, I wore designer clothes and carried designer bags. I was doing the "damn thang" and I felt that any man who wanted to be with me *HAD* to be of equal socioeconomic ranking. The man that wanted my heart had to be able to give me all the love, care, respect, admiration, commitment, and financial stability I deserved. To settle meant betraying everything I grew up believing in—abandoning those ideals that had become my standards for life, ignoring my moral compass, and surrendering my expectations about life and relationships. I measured every man I knew against my "man-o-meter", and that included my friends' men, my sisters' men, and all other men. My "man-o-meter" determined whether men measured up to my high standards.

I was a tough cookie, but I wanted what I wanted. To me, it was unconscionable to think that I'd ever allow myself to accept mediocrity from a man I was involved with. I had my standards and had no plans to lower them. Frankly, most men I met could never measure up to even half my list. They all seemed to fall within the 20-30% range, which was an unacceptable ratio for any man who wanted to be my mate. I couldn't understand other women who didn't subscribe to my relationship philosophy. I couldn't understand why they didn't demand more from a man yet complained when their relationships failed.

I was critical of everyone else's relationships and always found reasons to fault them. I judged my friends and their men and made my opinions very clear about what I would and wouldn't accept from a man, how I wouldn't take care of a man, and what I wouldn't allow my man to do. I thought my girlfriends were stupid, silly women with low-self-esteem. Essentially, everything a single woman says until she's in a relationship.

My friends Tamika, Sheila, Stephanie, and Jasmine were all in relationships with men I believed weren't their income equals. Tamika was a lawyer, Sheila was the VP of Finance for her company, Stephanie was a nurse practitioner, and Jasmine was a speech and language pathologist—all highly-skilled, successful women. They all had it going on, but their men left a lot to be desired, at least in my eyes. Tamika was married to a bank teller. Sheila's boyfriend was a patient registrar. Stephanie's boyfriend was a short-order cook for a restaurant, and Jasmine's husband was a shipping and receiving clerk. To me, they all seemed unworthy compared to my friends. Clearly, my friends earned more money than their significant others, so I just couldn't understand how these relationships could work.

I thought my friends were selling themselves short by dating or marrying men who couldn't afford to buy their own homes and moved in with my friends. Sometimes, my girls had to give money to their men until they got their next paychecks. Nope, I was determined that wouldn't be me. At times, I was downright disrespectful. I believed my girls were broken because their expectations and standards seemed to be so low. I, of course, always had something to say and couldn't hold my tongue. I got into huge screaming matches with my friends over this, but I just wanted the best for them. In my opinion, their choices in men didn't reflect women who loved themselves.

Little did I know, when I met Jason, I'd come to eat every judgmental word I'd ever uttered and every critical thought I'd ever had about my friends and their relationships. I had no idea that my time with Jason would be worse than anything I observed about my girlfriends' or my family's relationships and that I'd regret my words. Yes, the woman with so much to say about people's relationships, who spewed out so much judgment, fell in love with a man who couldn't hold a candle to any of her friends' men. I fell for a man I should never have considered, but for some reason, I was drawn to his "potential". Looking back, I'm not sure now if I ever thought he had potential. I think "potential" was justification for my acceptance of Jason and my desire to be with him.

Jason and I met in high school. We were good friends—at least for the first two years. In our third year, Jason was kicked out of school for stealing a teacher's credit card. He used the card to purchase food, beer, and liquor for one of the wild after-school parties he and his friends liked to throw. After he was expelled, he enrolled in another high school where he was suspended thirteen times before he eventually decided to drop out during his senior year. Jason had been something special to me. I used to call him "White Chocolate" because he was the coolest white boy I'd ever known! We spent many Friday nights together smoking weed, listening to music, or using phony IDs to get into the local clubs. We lost touch after I graduated and went to college, but we reconnected one day while I was home for a short visit.

I remember standing in line in the seafood department at the farmer's market. When my number was called, I asked the gentleman behind the counter for a couple of pieces of salmon. While waiting for my order, I heard a deep voice behind me say, "I like salmon too." I looked around and, to my surprise, I saw the voice belonged to Jason, my White Chocolate. We gave each other a quick hug, and what an affectionate hug it was! When we were in school Jason wasn't too tall, but he wasn't short either. He was actually kind of a funky-looking guy with long hair that he wore in a ponytail. Tattoos covered both of his arms, he wore an earring in one ear, and he had an eclectic dress style that set him apart from the other boys in school. Looking at him there in the grocery store, I noticed that his appearance had truly changed. He'd filled out nicely. He was no longer that skinny boy I used to hang with. Now, he was a muscle-bound, tattooed, sexy, fine-assed man. He rocked short hair and the earring was gone. Damn! He looked good enough to eat!

Normally, I never would have considered hooking up with a white boy. Well, let me be honest, I'll admit I've have drooled over and considered marriage with Justin Timberlake, Robert Downey, Jr., Brad Pitt, and George Clooney. But I'm getting off track. Back to Jason. To say he looked like a stallion was an understatement. I always knew he liked me, but I never gave him the time of day. I always kept him in the *friend zone*, but after seeing him that day, he quickly zoomed from the friend zone to the fuck zone. I wanted to ride that horsey! It was clear he was feeling me too. I saw him now as a grown man with an edge, which was a real turn-on. The connection between us was electric. We got together that night, and yes, we had sex. We didn't waste any time and I'm happy we didn't! The sex was great! From that night on, we were glued to each other. During the rest of my visit home, when I wasn't with friends or family, I was with Jason. We had so much fun I felt like we were reliving our high school years. Jason and I did things we hadn't done in a long time. I hadn't smoked marijuana in years, but Jason persuaded me to smoke with him.

It felt wonderful. I felt so relaxed and free from my dull routine of work. The release was something I needed—simple, stress-free fun. I was drinking, smoking, and Jason was snorting cocaine, something I never indulged in, but I knew that was his thing. He created an experience I hadn't enjoyed with anyone, not even my friends, for quite a while. When it was time to return home, I was a little sad because I didn't want my time with him to end and he didn't want me to leave. We agreed to see each other soon, which began with Jason visiting me at my home.

Two weeks later, he drove 2½ hours to see me. He was supposed to stay for the weekend, but it extended to a full week together. Our time together was filled with sex, drinking, and getting high. Again, things I hadn't indulged in for a long time. Typically, I might have a glass of wine. To drink and smoke every day wasn't my thing, but Jason persuaded me once again to relax and let go.

When Jason left, he returned three weeks later for a short visit that turned into a month-long stay. Things moved quickly from that point. Soon, we were in a relationship and Jason's third visit became permanent. Within five months, we were living together, and within one year, we were married.

My family and friends were shocked that I married Jason after only a year. They couldn't believe I married someone without a job, who came straight from a rented room in his aunt's house, and owned a ten-year-old hand-me-down car. Never mind coming close to checking off any of the boxes on my extensive list of standards and "must-haves" for the man I wanted to marry. In their eyes, I married a man who brought nothing to the table except good looks. And that's why I never told anyone about Jason's drug habit. I didn't need my family preaching more negativity about Jason. He was a good man with a good heart. He simply wasn't the "type of guy" my family thought I should be with.

Contrary to what my family believed, Jason had a job when we first got together. He was an environmental services worker at a local hospital, but he lost his job before he moved in with me. He'd been accused of stealing from some of the offices but the hospital was unable to prove anything, so the case was dropped. I wasn't worried about him getting another job because he was a hustler. He always ran a scam. Whether it was drugs or gambling, he found a way to get money. I saw the potential in him to channel that drive and enthusiasm from the street to a company. However, my family didn't feel the same way. They didn't consider him worthy of me and couldn't see his potential. They only supported our marriage because they loved me.

I was determined to prove my family wrong. I knew with my help Jason had the potential to accomplish whatever *I* believe he could. I had to do everything in my power to turn this man into the man I desired, so he became a project that eventually blew up in my face.

My first thought was to not pressure him to get a job right away. He'd just moved to a new city, and I knew it would take some time for him to find a job. Besides, I could support us both. I wanted him to get used to our new life. For the first three months of our marriage, we lived in a state of bliss. All we did was have sex, drink, and smoke marijuana. I didn't realize I was getting high with Jason so much until one day when I met my girlfriend for a quick lunch. She commented that my clothes smelled like weed. I was shocked! I never realized my clothes had a smell other than whatever fragrance I wore that day. I admitted that I'd been smoking with Jason, but she couldn't believe it. All my friends knew I didn't smoke. I'd have a drink sometimes, but I hadn't smoked since I was a teenager.

My friend asked what was going on that drove me to smoke. I told her nothing was going on. Jason smoked daily and liked me to join him. She was even more shocked to hear that and asked why he smoked every day. I told her it was no big deal. It was his way of relaxing after work. Then she asked a question I hoped she'd forgotten about, which was whether he was still unemployed. Head down, I admitted he was. She continued to grill me about why he'd smoke to relax when I was the one working and the one who should be relaxing. She was concerned about how I was changing, and she didn't like that I was drinking and smoking every day.

I could only sit there uncomfortably, imagining her response if I told her Jason also frequently snorted cocaine. I didn't like it, but he had it under control. That night when I got home, I was disturbed by my conversation with my friend, so when Jason started smoking and passed a joint to me, I refused. He was bewildered and asked if I was okay. I told him I was, but that I'd smoked more in the past year than I had in high school and college. He persisted and told me it was no big deal. Everyone smoked and he pressured me to take a hit or two with him. I couldn't resist and ended the night smoking and drinking.

The next morning, I woke up exhausted and dragged myself into work. I hadn't felt so terrible in a long time and it was impossible to concentrate. I decided I couldn't continue to drink and smoke like this. Jason didn't have a job so he could afford to sleep all day, but I didn't have that luxury. When I got home, I told Jason I wasn't drinking and smoking, but it didn't make a difference because he'd already started drinking and snorting cocaine before I got home. He had a party going on by himself. Music was playing and he was having a good time. All I wanted to do was take a shower and go to bed, but he wanted me to spend time with him. He wasn't happy that I wasn't getting high, but he let it go. I did try to stay awake to spend some time with him, but I was too exhausted to stay up long.

When I woke up in the middle of the night, Jason was gone. I was frantic with worry. I tried calling him, but it went straight to voicemail. An hour later, Jason stumbled through the door and barely made it to the bedroom before collapsing onto the bed. I was furious to see how drunk he was! Instead of my husband, all I saw was a loser who couldn't control himself. The next day, he was still sleeping when I went to work still fuming. My mind was a vortex of doubts and concerns. Had I made the biggest mistake of my life marrying Jason?

When I look back now, I can't imagine what happened to me. Why did I start a relationship with Jason? A bigger question is why would I *marry* him? I knew if one of my girlfriends asked my opinion about marrying a man like Jason, I'd have most certainly told her not to marry him. Moreover, if one of my nieces or godchildren asked me if she should marry a man with no job, money, and who couldn't take care of himself, I'd strongly discourage them. If that was my good advice for friends and family, why did I blindly refuse to heed the same for myself? I guess I wasn't focused on the reality of the marriage. Instead, I focused on his potential. I honestly thought I could bring him up to a level that met the standards on my wish list. I think it was Jason's street-savvy hustler image that reeled me in.

I saw him as a strong and confident man who walked to his own beat, and I loved it. I knew my friends and family felt something wasn't quite right with Jason mentally, but I was convinced he was just being himself.

In school, some of the kids called him Crazy Jason because he did some outrageous things, but we were kids and being "crazy" was cool. As kids, we saw him as someone who wasn't afraid to try anything but to adults, that kind of behavior was suspect and my friends and family saw Jason as someone to keep an eye on. They never said anything to me directly, but they silently shook their heads in bewilderment when he did something that concerned them. No one had the guts to say anything to me. Occasionally, people asked me about our relationship to try to understand it, but their cautious concern didn't affect me because I was determined to be with Jason whether they liked it or not. They didn't see him the way I did. I was convinced I could push him and change who he was.

I must admit Jason wasn't that smart. He never finished high school, and when he *was* in school, he never paid much attention to the teachers or his lessons. I think the teachers passed him because they wanted him out of their classrooms. They didn't care about him at all. I never looked down on Jason because of his limited education. I convinced myself that he was self-educated and that we were on the same intellectual level, but deep inside I was nervous when he opened his mouth around my friends. I always defended him, but the words I used in his defense were simply lies.

When we hung out with my friends and their men, we inevitably ended up having intense conversations on a wide variety of topics. I was anxious the entire time because I never knew what would come out of Jason's mouth. More often than not, the crazy comments he contributed to the conversations left me embarrassed and ashamed of him. When we were out in public, things were worse. The way he dressed started to become an issue for me. At first, I thought he was just eclectic, but I soon started to hate the way he dressed. I found myself telling him what clothes to wear and how he should wear them. I was functioning as his mother instead of his woman. He was nothing like the independent, accomplished man I always expected to marry.

Jason eventually got a job six months after we got married, but he never seemed to be able to keep it. After a month or two, something always happened. There were plenty of suitable job opportunities but he turned them down for one reason or another. I guess he felt free to pick and choose because no matter what, he knew the bills would be paid. *I* was taking care of *him*. I was in rescue mode and determined to save him.

My attempt to save Jason and turn him into a different man was more taxing than enriching. I took care of him and provided whatever he needed. I bought him a car, paid for his health coverage, gave him access to my bank accounts, and didn't pressure him to get a job. My actions only reinforced his total lack of ambition and drive and his inability to contribute to our life together. I tried everything I could think of to help turn Jason into the man I wanted, but the more I tried to change him, the angrier he became, and the more he drank, smoked, and snorted cocaine. He hated that I was trying to turn him into someone else. He wondered why I married him if I didn't like him the way he was. I must admit, *that* was an excellent question. Most of the time, I told Jason what to do and when to do it. He didn't like it, but I hated it as much as he did. I didn't want to keep instructing a grown man on how to act. We argued all the time. He begged me to stop telling him what to do, but I couldn't help myself.

One night we got into a heated argument because I simply asked him to take out the trash if he noticed the trash can overflowing. Instead of expressing his feelings, he picked up a vase and threw it at the wall. I knew right then that things had to change. He couldn't continue to blow up and smash things against the wall because, in my mind, throwing things could easily escalate into hitting things and I didn't want to become the object of choice.

When Jason threw that vase, I was somewhat frightened but not shocked because I was familiar with his temper. He had a short fuse and blew up in an instant. But this latest incident reminded me that I'd willingly chosen to be with him fully aware of who he was. I also knew I had to choose whether to stay with him and deal with his anger issues or if it was time to leave. Of course, once he apologized and kissed me, my resistance immediately faded along with my decision. All I could focus on was how to make things better for Jason. I felt compelled to act by channeling my efforts into finding him a job because I believed his frustration stemmed from his unemployment.

I started searching for jobs for Jason. I asked my friends to hook him up and they did, all on the strength of their love for me. My cousin worked in a pharmaceutical manufacturing company that happened to have several openings for packers. I was so relieved when she told me it would be easy for Jason to get one of those jobs. She got him an interview and he was offered the job on the spot. After working only one week, I saw a dramatic improvement in Jason's attitude. I was finally happy, and *he* was happy, too. Our relationship improved because he was contributing something to our household. It wasn't as much as I would have liked, but at least he had an income. Now I could proudly tell my family and friends that my man had a job. Yes!

Secretly I was happy because Jason had to stop smoking, drinking, and snorting cocaine because his job conducted random drug screenings and if he had positive results, he'd lose his job. To get through the pre-employment drug screening, he had me pee into a cup. He poured it into a small vial and used it for his drug test. Of course, he passed because I stopped smoking with him a few weeks before he got the job.

Four months after Jason started working at the manufacturing company, I found out I was pregnant with twins. Jason was excited. He always wanted kids and now, at last, we were going to have not one, but two. He realized that things were going to change for our family. We were growing and that meant more expenses. Jason suddenly felt pressured to make more money so he could take care of his children. He took on extra hours to make as much money as possible before the twins arrived. I was so proud of him. He wasn't home a lot, but he was earning money for his family.

When the twins came, Jason bought everything they needed. I was so impressed with him that I couldn't help brag to my friends about everything he did for our children. I was elated to see how happy the children made him Jason. He showered me and the kids with gifts and was contributing more than his half to the household bills, which made me happy! Our financial situation was more stable now and our savings were growing. I went back to the checklist I created while I was still looking for the perfect man and finally began checking off boxes on my list. It just confirmed that our relationship was stronger and more solid than ever.

However, when the twins were about five months old, I started to notice a change in Jason's attitude. One moment he was cranky, the next he was angry, and some days he was just plain nasty. It was hard for us to have a conversation without him biting my head off. I knew things had changed at work. He wasn't getting as many hours as he had before the twins came, but he was working steadily.

I remember one Sunday afternoon after Jason returned from watching a football game at a local bar. It was obvious he'd been drinking. I asked him how much he had and he told me a couple of beers. I thought it was no big deal. He asked about the twins and went upstairs to see them. I stayed downstairs preparing food for the week and doing laundry. About half an hour after Jason went upstairs, I heard one of the babies crying. I didn't respond immediately because Jason was there, but after five minutes, I still heard the baby crying. I rushed upstairs and to my horror, one of the twins was on the floor. Jason passed out while holding my son. He slipped out of Jason's arms and fell. I ran to rescue my child. When I picked him up, I noticed a bleeding cut over his right eye.

I lost it. I screamed and kicked Jason into consciousness. I yelled, "You dropped the baby! You dropped the baby! He's bleeding. We have to go to the hospital!" Jason jumped up startled. It took him a moment to realize what I was saying. I rushed to dress the baby and shouted at Jason to get our other child. I was furious and terrified. Jason jumped in front of me screaming at me to calm down and demanded to see the baby. He tried to persuade me that our son was fine. I cleaned the blood from my baby's forehead to assess the injury. It wasn't as bad as it looked, but I still wanted to go to the hospital to get him checked. Jason told me to calm down and that the baby was fine. I told him I was taking our son to the hospital. He said if I told them what happened, they'd probably call child protective services.

The reality of his words sank in. Jason had drugs in his system. It was obvious what would happen if the medical staff found out. I didn't know he was still taking drugs, but I also didn't care. I was taking my son to the hospital. Of course, I had to answer their questions, but I lied and they believed me. My son was fine and didn't require stitches. I was grateful but furious with Jason. How could he be so reckless with our children?

When I got home, Jason and I got into the biggest argument of our relationship. I told him the situation could have been a disaster if the hospital learned the truth and that he better get himself together if he wanted to stay in our children's life. I was so concerned about my children I barely spoke to Jason for a week. He swore he wouldn't drink or do drugs anymore because the incident with our son terrified him and he knew he had to do better. I didn't believe him. Jason had a serious drug problem and I couldn't trust him with our children. I had a dilemma on my hands.

I delayed making any decisions about our relationship, but I knew I had to do something soon. Our relationship was rapidly deteriorating. Jason was staying out more often and wasn't home to help me with the children, but I didn't care because I couldn't trust him with them. One night I slept with the children in our bed. I was suddenly awakened by a noise coming from downstairs. I leaped out of bed and looked for Jason on the chaise lounge in our room, but he wasn't there. When I glanced at the clock, I saw that it was 4 am. I called out to Jason but there was no answer. Now I was scared. I reached for the knife I kept under the mattress. I closed the bedroom door and slowly crept downstairs. My heart was pounding with fear and anger. Scared that it may be an intruder, but furious that my husband wasn't home to protect his family.

When I got downstairs, I saw Jason peeling off his clothes and throwing them one item at a time across the room and knocking down items from the floating shelves near the television. He was clearly

TRUTH BE TOLD | ALETHEA TAYLOR

drunk. I asked him, "Didn't you hear me calling for you?" He didn't answer. I asked him where he'd been and why he'd come home so late. He answered, "I'm a grown man, I come home when I feel like it." I responded, "Yeah, but you're a grown and married man. Have some respect!" He replied, "Who the hell do you think you're talking to?" I told him, "I thought I was talking to you? Who else is here beside your family?" To my surprise, he said, "Bitch, you're not my mother. Stop questioning me!" I said, "Who are you calling a bitch? Your mother is a bitch!" He said, "Talk back to me again and I'm knocking your teeth out!" I looked at him with pure hatred. "Then get the fuck out!" I shouted. "I'm not taking your shit anymore!" He fired back, "I'm not going anywhere. This is my house too!" Not wanting to put my children at risk, I turned and went back upstairs.

With each step, my fear vanished but hurt permeated my heart. My husband called me a bitch and threatened to physically harm me. I was devastated. How could he be so cruel and hurtful? Clearly, his drug usage was taking a toll. When he wasn't high, he was a much calmer man, but when he couldn't get his fix, he became a monster. Secretly, I preferred him on drugs because I could tolerate him more. But that night he crossed the line. Going back to sleep was impossible. I

- 142 - | P a g e

cried into my pillow, mourning the end of my relationship. When I woke up the next morning, Jason was still there. I didn't have the stamina to risk another fight or worse by insisting he leave, so I simply ignored him for a week. He tried apologizing, but his empty promises to change his ways turned out to be meaningless.

Barely a month later, we faced another issue that became the turning point of our relationship. Jason came home early one evening and dinner wasn't ready. When he discovered there wasn't anything to eat, he went berserk! He stormed into the kitchen and started rummaging through the refrigerator looking for something to eat. He began throwing things out of the refrigerator and onto the floor, against the walls, into the sink, and at the cabinets. He had a complete meltdown. I screamed at him to stop and asked him what was wrong, but he continued to throw things. I asked him again to stop and told him he was scaring me and to calm down. He finally ran out of things to throw and started pacing the floor. He gripped his head and banged his fist against it saying, "How could this be happening? Someone ratted on me and I'm going to kill him!" I asked him what he was talking about. He said, "The people at work think I'm a part of a gang funneling drugs out of the company and now the police want to talk to me." I said, "Ok. You didn't do anything wrong, so you have nothing to worry about."

"You don't understand," he shouted. "You could never understand. This is a total fuck up!"

I didn't understand what he was talking about until two detectives showed up on our doorstep that night. Things got a lot clearer and more worrisome. There was a knock on the door while Jason was in the middle of telling me what happened at work. When he heard it, he whispered, "The cops! That's the police!" I thought Jason was losing it until I answered the door and two detectives asked for him. Jason rushed to the basement to hide. When the detectives asked to speak to him, I lied and told them he wasn't home yet. When they turned to leave, I quickly slammed the door and went downstairs to the basement. I demanded he tell me exactly what was going on—all of it. He told me to sit down and proceeded to tell me it was all true. He said he joined a team of men who moved drugs from the plant to buyers. He'd been fired four months ago when he was caught smuggling a bag of pills out of the warehouse.

To say I was shocked would be a huge understatement. He explained that even after he was fired, he continued to help move the drugs from the plant to the place where they were sold. The Feds had been watching him for some time and he was subject to even greater scrutiny because the company reported his activities to the police after he was fired. Selling drugs wasn't foreign to Jason. It was the reason he spent so much time in and out of jail. He'd been caught selling drugs—marijuana specifically—but this time he was stealing Viagra, pain pills, diet pills, and a host of other prescription drugs. While we were talking, the voice in my head said, *How could you have been so blind? How could you not know he wasn't working?* I told him he'd better haul his ass to the police and turn himself in. I warned him to tell them everything because I didn't want the police or detectives coming to my home again. As Jason continued with his story, things got worse. He said the police were the least of our worries and that some other people were after him. It seems the people he had been working with and the people he'd been selling to all wanted him. He believed someone from the drug ring had turned him in.

At this point, I was shaking with rage and confusion. Why would he put his family in harm's way? I ran to the bedroom to pack a few things, grabbed the twins, and headed for my mother's house. I was scared, angry, and felt like a fool. All these emotions overwhelmed me. It was like a mental tsunami. I called Jason as I drove to my mother's house and told him he'd better handle this situation quickly and make things right again. He repeatedly apologized for being such an idiot, but I just hung up. I didn't want to hear it. I didn't call Jason the next day. I didn't speak to him for three days because I couldn't stand the sound of his voice. When I did finally speak to him, he told me that he'd been arrested.

Jason was sentenced to four years in prison— four years away from his children, his wife, and his family. Do you want to talk about embarrassed? I was completely mortified. I tried to avoid my friends and family at all costs. My family thought Jason's prison sentence would surely be my wakeup call and that I'd leave him, but guess what? I didn't walk away. I waited for Jason. Yes, me! I waited—me, the woman who swore she'd never consider a man with a low-paying job, let alone a man with a drug problem and serving time in prison. But we had a family, and I felt it would be cruel to abandon him at his lowest moment. He was my husband and I was committed to him. During our wedding ceremony, the preacher asked both of us to recite, "For better or worse?" Well, this certainly had to be what he meant by "worse". All I knew was that I felt obligated to stand by my husband.

While Jason was in prison, I had time to gather my thoughts, recall my life goals, reflect on what was important to me, what was best for my children, and decide what I truly wanted in a man. I began keeping a journal, which was one of the best decisions I could have made to help me deal with a stressful situation. The journal provided the relief I needed to help me cope with the turmoil in my life. I wrote in it every day. I wrote whatever came to my mind—my feelings, thoughts, fears, aspirations, secrets, and my vision for the future. I sometimes wrote for hours but I never read it once I put my thoughts on paper. I wrote in that journal for the better part of three years before I decided to read it.

As I read what I wrote about Jason and me, I knew it was time to ask myself some tough questions. The most important question I had to tackle was, "Why I was holding onto Jason?" Clearly, he was incapable of being the man I needed in my life and wasn't a responsible father for our children. I understood he had felt like he did what he had to when he decided to sell drugs, but it was obvious he never thought about the consequences or potential harm that could have come to his family because of his poor judgment. His reckless behavior had no place in our lives. It couldn't be all about him anymore. I realized that he didn't comprehend the magnitude of his responsibilities as a husband and father.

For that reason, I decided once Jason was released from prison, I would file for divorce. I did not want to file while he was in jail because I knew his anger would push him to respond in a way that could possibly earn him more time behind bars. I didn't want that. He'd been away from our children long enough. As much as I knew Jason and I could no longer function as a couple, he was still my children's father and that would never change. Of course, he'd have to prove himself to me and our children that he'd put them and their welfare first and step up if he wanted to remain an active parent in their lives. However, as a family, I couldn't continue with a failed marriage.

Truth Be Told, my desire to be with Jason was based on the physical attraction I felt for him. I realize now that basing life decisions on physical attraction or looks is ridiculous. Those things can't be sustained, and they certainly aren't enough to support a lasting relationship. Years before reconnecting with Jason, I created a detailed laundry list of things I wanted from a man, but somehow the list went out the window once I bumped into him. Before Jason, I never understood why my friends saddled themselves with men who were far from their equals. I was bewildered and confused about why I did the same. I was an intelligent, educated woman who never suffered from low self-esteem. Had I truly been that gullible to fall for good looks alone when all the other warning signs were clearly there? I judged my friends, their men, their relationships, and boasted about how I'd never settle for a man who brought nothing to the relationship. I learned a lesson in humility I'd never forget.

Truth Be Told, I realize now that you never know how you'll react to a situation until you face it yourself. It was wrong for me to judge my friends and their relationships. I had no right to judge them or anyone else, but I allowed my arrogance to dictate my actions. I've learned that what works for one person's relationship may not work for another's. We all have different wants and needs and to project our desires on other people is wrong. It's also a mistake to try to change someone to suit your needs. **Truth Be Told**, I knew all along that Jason was far from the man I truly desired. It was impossible to mold him into someone he wasn't simply to make him fit into my unrealistic expectations.

  Truth Be Told, my plan to change Jason backfired. Instead of me changing him, he changed me. I settled. I lowered my expectations just to be with him even though deep in my heart I knew I was making a mistake. No, I didn't believe I was better than Jason. We simply never shared the same goals, ambitions, or work ethics. Our passion for life was so far out of sync there was no way we could realistically mesh.

  While Jason and I remain, friends, I've learned that it's important to walk away from any person or relationship when it doesn't measure up to your needs and desires from the relationship. **Truth Be Told**, I couldn't change Jason into someone he wasn't capable of being. I've learned you must accept people for who they are, and who they are may not necessarily be the right person for a relationship. Seeing potential in someone comes from your perspective only. It doesn't mean they'll recognize it within themselves. There comes a time when you must accept that you can't bring people to the level *you* believe they're capable of. Only they can do that. Yes, you can encourage them, you can support and guide them, but that desire must stem from their heart and soul. If not, you're only building a house of sand destined to crumble.

Truth Be Told, and lesson learned, don't be fooled by superficial feelings or physical attraction. Take control of your emotions and think before making hasty decisions. It's an old saying, but it's true. Everything that glitters isn't gold. Dig beneath the surface because the core is where you live. Just because something makes you feel good for the moment doesn't mean it's the best decision for you long-term.

CHAPTER SEVEN

Bailey

A Letter to Singleness

I'm single, and I love it! Why should I be ashamed of being single? There's nothing wrong with being single. I'm living in my singleness, and I'm walking through it with my head held high.

Singleness, I fear you no more. Never again will I be afraid to carry you, no more will I be afraid to embrace you, and no longer will I be afraid to shout that you're *my* friend. There's such a stigma associated with being your friend. You're seen as an incurable disease, so people question why anyone would want to associate with you. They wonder how such a relationship can possibly exist in a world where "single" is essentially defined as a dirty word. They perceive you as a pariah, an uncomfortable question mark in a society built on the hallowed foundations of "we" or "us". People look at you differently, they glance sideways at you, and whisper behind your back simply because you're not with the program. Your independence threatens them. You make them uncomfortable by forcing them to look at themselves in ways they'd rather not. So, you became my secret. I locked you away like a dusty old diary and hid the key. I pushed you away. I was too afraid to hold your hand. I shied away from your embrace. I couldn't even utter your name, let alone acknowledge your existence. For that, I owe you a heartfelt apology, Singleness.

The journey of embracing you wasn't always an easy one. Initially, I didn't want to get to know you. I avoided you as long as possible. Certainly, I didn't want you looking at me, speaking to me, and I definitely didn't want you dropping by my place, knocking on my door, and introducing yourself to me. Like a battered childhood toy I couldn't bear to surrender, I wanted to cling to my friendship with my other friend, Relationship. It didn't matter how Relationship mistreated me. I didn't care about the tears or the permanent ache in my heart. I was determined not to become your friend. I wanted to maintain my friendship with Relationship, even though Relationship disrespected me, even though Relationship had many other friends, even though Relationship called me a bitch until I almost forgot my real name. I still wanted to be friends with Relationship regardless of the toll it took on my soul. Anything was better than having you as my friend.

The mere thought of you caused me to experience intense anxiety. You were the noise in the hallway at night no one had the courage to check. What I knew of you was the spawn of pity and nightmares. I judged you based on the words of others and witnessing the sad fate of those you befriended. Some sank into depression. Others felt the sting of grief because they despised your friendship. They hid in dark places and covered their eyes to avoid your friendship. Why would anyone want to know you? Others perceived you as a vampire ready to suck the life from them. They looked at you and saw hopelessness and despair.

However, to my surprise, you were the refreshing breath of fresh air I needed blown into my life. As they say, you can't judge a book by its cover, and by turning the page on our friendship, we wrote healing chapters for what became my reborn attitude and perspective on life. I realized how badly you'd also been mistreated and misunderstood. You weren't the devil in the dark after all. You were that transition between the darkness of night and the welcome light of dawn. You were more than a friend. You became my blood, my soul, and more importantly, you became *me*.

In the beginning, our friendship had many ups and downs. I'm ashamed to admit I screamed and hollered at you, cried over you, and denied your existence, but like a loyal pet, you waited patiently. You refused to let me go and continued to demonstrate what a loving and compassionate friend you were. I was stubborn. I didn't want your friendship. You were a loser in my eyes, and to be friends with you meant admitting I was too. I preferred to wallow in my own self-pity and beliefs that I was undesirable, which was something you refused to allow me to accept. You were persistent. You never gave up on me despite my resistance. Slowly, like the ever-fanning ripples on a pond, I began to welcome your presence. I understood you were there to help me, to comfort me, and that you couldn't wait to show me how wonderful our friendship could be.

So I threw open the curtains and allowed the sun to shine on my face. I wiped away my tears and welcomed you as my friend. Once I got to know you and experienced the joy, freedom, and excitement of our friendship, I felt as though the shackles binding me for so long had shattered. Like explorers stumbling upon a priceless artifact, we explored the awesome things about me that made me so unique, that made me so *me*. I learned to know what I liked and what I didn't like. You helped me make a list of the qualities I was searching for in a man and what I wouldn't accept from a man. Most importantly, I learned to focus my love on only me and enjoy without guilt this process of self-discovery.

I spent time doing what I needed and wanted without asking anybody's permission or getting their approval about my activities. With you, I could finally relax and do what I always wanted to do when and how I wanted. I didn't have to hear that nagging voice in my ear asking what I was doing, offering their opinions, responding with anger, or challenging my decisions. I spent time with you free from the burden of catering to others, and what a joy that was! To finally surrender to you was your ultimate gift to me.

Through my revelation, I eventually embraced you. I loved you with a passion that blazed like the summer sun. I adored you because you helped me discover that you were never the monster others portrayed you to be. You were my guardian angel. But, there were times I grew weary of having only you as my friend. The desire for additional friends crept up on me, and I felt a sense of anxiety because no one else was around. This anxiety revealed to me that I wasn't truly at peace with just us.

However, after three years, or maybe it was four, I was at peace with you. I no longer worried about you being my only friend, and that's when other friends came knocking at my door. When old Relationship sought me out, and even when new Relationship wanted to be my friend, I was so content with you, Singleness, that I wasn't sure if I even wanted Relationship as my friend. I learned so much from you, Singleness. I nurtured my strength, my confidence, my independence. I rediscovered the love I had for myself, and most of all, I started to live more abundantly because I embraced you as my friend. You brought joy to my life, you forced me to think about what was important to me, and what made me happy — all necessary steps to prepare me for the time you give your blessing to me and my new friend, Relationship.

Truth Be Told, Singleness, I'm a better person because of you. You, my beloved friend, were the best thing that ever happened to me! I'm filled with gratitude for our time together and will cherish our friendship until I'm confident about befriending Relationship again. Singleness, I love you. I appreciate you more than you know. I'm truly blessed to call you *friend*.

CHAPTER EIGHT

Madison

It's Ok to Leave

I wanted to leave for a long time, but the time never seemed right. I sacrificed, I cried, I endured, and I planned for my departure. My childhood aspirations inspired me and triggered an emotional awakening that led to an epiphany that my marriage vows to "forsake all others", didn't equate to forsaking my happiness and that I was condemned to endure a life sentence of misery and despair. I left, and it was the best decision I could have made, for ME!

Paul and I raised four beautiful children together, but once the first three went to college and only our youngest daughter remained at home with us, there wasn't much for me to do anymore. My life was no longer as hectic. I didn't have to oversee homework, drive kids around, do laundry for six people, or cook dinner for the kids and all their friends. Things were slowing down. Suddenly, I no longer had the welcome distractions that had kept me from facing the miserable life that enshrouded me like a spiderweb. Our children and their numerous extra-curricular activities kept me more than busy and served as barriers that helped me cope with my husband. I was committed to staying in my marriage, but when the children slowly began to explore the new-found independence that came with young adulthood, the barren desert that was my life became a prison. The children usually only visited on holidays and I was left with more time on my hands than I knew how to handle. Gone was the fortress of activities that shielded my sanity. Instead, I was left with too much time to think about my life and whether I really wanted to stay trapped in a marriage to a man I no longer loved. If it hadn't been for our children, our relationship would have been over long ago. I remember looking at Paul one day and thinking, "I don't even know if I like him—I love him as the father of my children, but I don't think I *like* him."

Over the years, countless confrontations occurred between Paul and me. Our yelling and screaming matches surpassed typical arguments. These were disrespectful, venomous disagreements. I was always mindful that he was my husband and that there were some things I'd never vocalize. However, for him, nothing was off-limits when he was in a rage. He said some cruel and hurtful things to me as though I were some random stranger that had picked a fight. I recall one time, in the midst of one of our battles, Paul shouted, "Fuck you!" I was in shock. I couldn't believe he'd say such a horrible thing to me. The words replayed in my mind like an endless litany. How could he say that to me? When I heard those words, they felt like a sucker punch to the chest. I was physically and mentally wounded. I was crushed! I understood that arguments happened even in the best marriages, but I believed that a husband and wife should be respectful and considerate of how they spoke to one another.

It was a bitter lesson that taught me there were certain lines that shouldn't be maliciously crossed. It was painfully clear that Paul didn't have the same beliefs. Like a Rottweiler, he went for the jugular every time and I was left feeling like a savaged victim. His disregard for my feelings during those angry encounters resulted in a mental disconnect with him. While physical abuse can leave visible scars, verbal abuse can be just as damaging. We were polite and fun-loving in front of family members and our friends, but it was all an act.

The constant turmoil between us destroyed any romantic feelings and ultimately caused me to fall out of love with Paul. We lost the romance and any sense of connection. We slept in separate bedrooms because there was no need to share a bed—sex was a distant memory. I no longer had any desire for him, and I had no intention of trying to rekindle something that I was convinced was forever gone. After twenty-eight years of marriage, the journey that began on a smooth road forked into two distant, rocky paths. I couldn't bear staying with the man he'd become. Our values and perspectives were completely different. As Paul grew older, his beliefs and standards became nearly diabolical. The rage festering within him erupted in his every response. I was the opposite. Regardless of how angry I was, I was always mindful that he was my husband and the father of my children. I learned to tread lightly and not disrespect him, but it was a challenge! Paul viewed things through one set of lenses and I through another.

Truth Be Told, I believe our opposing views were always part of our relationship. When I was a young, naïve new bride, it never occurred to me that our differences would prove toxic to our relationship. I thought they balanced us. Of course, there were things Paul didn't like about me, and there were things I didn't like about him, but we thought love would eventually conquer any issues we might encounter. These little things weren't deal breakers for either of us, so I chose to focus more on the things I *did* like about him. We shared plenty of things in common—we liked the same foods, rooted for the same football teams, and we liked to hike and ski. There were many activities we enjoyed doing and we had wonderful times together. Nevertheless, over the years, we both changed, and the relationship became increasingly difficult to hold together. Now, we had virtually nothing in common other than a desire to fuss and argue all the time.

Most of our arguments involved sex. As we grew older, our sexual desires and drive changed. Paul experienced an increased sex drive while mine decreased. The decline in my sexual desire wasn't age-related. I was simply no longer attracted to my husband. I couldn't connect with him anymore on any level. I am, and always have been, the type of woman who needs to connect with a man mentally before I can connect physically. For me, lovemaking begins with mental stimulation, which serves as foreplay. I've always considered men more visual while I'm more psychological. The problem was that now the only mental picture I had of him was yelling and screaming at me and the kids. It created a massive roadblock in my mind. To be fair, Paul always had an insatiable sexual appetite and that stayed consistent throughout the early years of our marriage, but somewhere along the line, his sexual appetite increased. I don't know whether it was a reaction from all the supplements he was taking, but I simply wasn't interested in satisfying his sexual needs in any way.

Truth Be Told, from the beginning, our sex desires were always slightly out of sync. We had sex regularly. However, he knew I wasn't particularly excited about it. I liked sex, but I didn't need it all the time. I always thought that Paul's sex drive would slow

down once we got married, you know, once the novelty
wore off. I had no idea that sex would become such a
big deal. Many of my girlfriends who'd been married
for a while warned me that after we were married, sex
wouldn't be nearly as important as it was before
marriage. So, there we were. I had this nice-looking
man that was all mine. We made a beautiful couple.
Paul wanted to marry me. I wanted to marry him. We
were young and excited and never gave any thought to
what marriage might be like after the initial glow wore
off. Any thoughts I may have had about a decline in my
husband's sex drive were just thoughts. The man never
let up.

Everything was about sex. As I look back,
maybe I would have been more interested in sex if it
had been about US. Instead, it was always all about
Paul. When he wanted it. How he wanted it. His focus
was only on his desires, never mine. Often, when I'd be
asleep after a grueling day dealing with the kids, he
woke me because his hard dick demanded attention.
Pleasing me was the furthest thing from his mind. I
might as well have been a blow-up doll for all he cared.
His only concern was that I pleased him. There were
times when I thought he just needed an obliging hole
to stick his dick into rather than any actual desire to
make love to his wife. It made me feel cheap and
worthless. When Paul got angry with me because I
refused to have sex with him, he told me he knew

where he could find some "good pussy". He said it so often I started to believe that he was either having an affair or referring to his ex-girlfriend.

Before we married, Paul had been seeing another woman while he was seeing me. I knew about it, knew he was in love with her, and I even knew they had an unbelievable sex life. He said she was the best sex partner he'd ever had. Despite their torrid sex life, he decided I was the one he wanted to marry. He chose me, but I think he always second-guessed whether he made the right decision. I knew he kept in touch with her over the years, and I think they may have even had an affair, but I couldn't prove it. Paul never realized that I knew they kept in touch. Once, when I asked about her, he said they were still friends, but she lived in another city and that I didn't need to worry about her. Still, I was convinced that when he said he was going to visit friends, he was going to see her. His need to stay connected to this woman led me to believe that he still had feelings for her, that maybe he'd like to explore a relationship with her, but because of our children, he stayed with me. It made no difference that I couldn't prove any of this. We'd become obligations to each other rather than partners.

The rest of our arguments focused primarily on what was suitable or acceptable for our children. Paul thought I was too soft on them, and I thought he was too harsh. The kids often came to me in tears because

their dad yelled at them. His anger was terrifying, and
they were afraid of him. That was no way for kids to
live. Don't misunderstand, I expected our children to
have a healthy fear of both of us, but I wanted them to
fear a stern reprimand for disobeying us, not fear that
we might hit them. I thought I was doing a good job of
concealing my fear regarding my husband, but I finally
realized that our children knew I was afraid, so they
also grew to fear him.

I knew a lot of Paul's anger stemmed from his
frustration with our marriage. I was just as frustrated as
he was, but my anger looked different. He was
constantly disrespectful to me. He didn't treat me like
his wife or the mother of his children. Instead, he
called me names and seemed to be angry with me all
the time. My kids watched as he made me cry. When I
ran to my bedroom in tears, they got involved. They
were angry with him because he made Mommy cry.
When that happened, he focused his anger on the
children, yelling at them and threatening to harm
them—something he believed he had every right to do.
I'd quickly pull myself together and try to calm him
down *for their sake*. I believe Paul thought he could yell
and scream at us over every little thing because he took
care of us. God forbid we touch or move anything of
his. That would trigger him for sure. At times, we felt
like we couldn't be ourselves. We tiptoed around
careful not to upset him. Our home was no longer a

warm, relaxing haven. It had become a war zone. Paul and I were enemies staring each other down from different sides. I quickly grew tired of his treatment and began to despise him!

Every time he made me cry, every time he made my children cry, I wanted to leave. Once things cooled down, the children went back to being their childlike, happy selves, content with both of their parents. While the kids were quick to bounce back from Paul's blow-ups, I stored everything in the back of my mind. I kept a secret mental lockbox where I squirreled away all the hurt, pain, and disappointment we endured. Once those feelings were safely tucked away, I continued like everything was fine. I did this because I didn't want to disrupt my children's lives. I'd grown up with two loving parents and I didn't want to deny my children the benefits of being raised in a two-parent household, so I stuck it out for them. Despite Paul's flaws, and as much as I hate to admit it, he did take care of us. He worked hard to provide for us. We had a great house, multiple cars, and all the newest in electronics and modern technology. You name it, we had it. He made sure that once our children were old enough to drive and they got their driver's licenses, each had their own car. He paid all the bills, paid for our children's college tuition, and made sure I had all the material things I could ever want. He provided for us as I expected any good father and husband to do, but still, we continuously bumped heads. We were like oil and water, fire and ice.

The more the turmoil in our marriage continued to escalate, the more frustrated and hopeless I felt. I didn't know what to do to make things better, but I did know that I needed to scream, to cry, I needed whatever it would take to release all my pent-up disappointment, hurt, and fear. I needed to purge everything because those emotions were engulfing my body like a tsunami. It felt like a raging fire in my belly. I can't actually describe what I felt except that I was dying a slow, agonizing death. The effort and energy it took to put on a brave face for everyone else's benefit were becoming too much. I was living for everyone else. I didn't want others to think I was a failure because I couldn't keep my marriage together, so I suffered in silence just to save face. Sadly, my life had become about everyone but me!

I was slowly drowning in despair until the day I went searching for a few serving trays my sister had been asking me to bring over for our annual family reunion. The trays were stored in my basement for safekeeping. As I started opening boxes in search of the trays, I found a box of things from my school days. It was filled with my old school essays, yearbooks, pictures, etc. Distracted from my search, I began digging through the box. I pulled out a letter I'd written when I was in the 6th grade. The letter talked about my future goals and what I wanted to be when I grew up. I pulled out more letters and essays and drifted back in time as I read them. Soon, I found myself crying, laughing, and then crying again. I felt an immense sense of release and sadness, joy, and encouragement. Another letter, also from 6th grade, described how much I enjoyed taking walks in the park and collecting the bright, crisp colored fall leaves. How I longed to once again enjoy those simple, long-forgotten childhood pleasures.

It was at that very moment, as I read those messages from my 6th-grade self, that I experienced an epiphany. Rediscovering my young self had given me strength. I realized I was spending too much time making everyone else happy at the expense of my own happiness. Sitting there on the hard, cold floor of my basement with tears of joy streaming down my face and snot running from my nose, I kissed those letters from my childhood and vowed not to continue suffering for the sake of others. I needed to do something for me. I needed to live! In that time of reflection, I also knew that to live, I had to leave my marriage, so I set out to do just that.

It's amazing how something as random as finding a box of old letters would change my life, but **Truth Be Told**, finding the letters wasn't a coincidence. It was an intervention, a saving grace, a call to action. They gave me the courage and determination, after twenty-eight years, to finally admit I'd had enough and to be sure he knew I meant it! I carried those letters with me every day. They were a constant reminder of what was really important in life and a source of strength that kept pushing me forward. With hope fueling my actions, I devised an exit plan to free me from my dysfunctional marriage. I wanted to be sure I had all my ducks in a row so I'd be ready and well-prepared to start a new life on my own. I did everything I could think of to make this transition a smooth one. I carefully thought about what I wanted out of the divorce. Did I want to keep our home or look for a new one? Maybe I should sell the house and split the proceeds with Paul. I considered how we'd divide our other possessions. I spent my days searching for a condo and a job. I mapped out how I'd support myself and I thought long and hard about how to tell my children I was leaving their father. I considered every possible aspect of my decision so when the time came to exit, I could boldly embrace this journey to my new life.

I finally decided it was time to share my decision with my closest family members and good friends. As expected, most of them were completely shocked. Many of them questioned my decision to leave. They kept repeating, "But you've been together for twenty-eight years." Was it possible they really believed I should continue to stay in a broken marriage solely on the merit of longevity? A few of my friends tried scare tactics by telling me there were no good single men around and I might end up all alone. They tried to convince me I'd be better off if I stayed with the man I had. Another group of friends thought I'd lost my mind. They thought I was being irrational, that it was insane to leave Paul after spending so many years building our lives together. What they didn't seem to realize was that I *was* in my right mind. I thought long and hard about my decision, and when I finally made it, it gave me the first sense of peace I'd felt in years. Well-intentioned people kept telling me that marriage was hard, that I just had to get through this rough patch, but to me, it wasn't just a "rough patch", it was a *prison…and yes,* the *prison* of life trapped in a suffocating, invisible cage was brutal. I'd taken solemn vows but I hadn't heard the minister say anything about a prison sentence being part of those vows. I arrived at the church eager to start my marriage. I was filled with hope and happiness, but the reality was that most of the time my marriage was filled with helplessness and hopelessness. When people asked, "How could you decide to leave after 28 years?" I replied, "Why shouldn't I?" I was viewing my life through a lens that was vastly different from theirs. From my perspective, *they* were the crazy ones, not me.

Why do some people find it so shocking when someone decides to leave a bad relationship regardless of the length of time spent together? It's baffling to me that others have such a difficult time accepting that a relationship is over. Perhaps it's a reflection of their fears and insecurities about their own relationship. The hard truth was that I stayed in my marriage because of my children, but now it was simply over. Our marriage was dead. Paul and I were more like business associates than lovers, husband and wife, or life partners, and I found that both disappointing and unacceptable. I didn't want a marriage that felt like a business deal. I wanted romance. I wanted passion. I wanted to *feel* something special. But as time passed, passion retreated like a mirage forever taunting me from a distant horizon. Before we got married, we were told there would be times when we'd have to fight through some tough situations to keep our marriage together, that marriages had ups and downs but that we could always find our way back to each other.

What people failed to tell us was that battles within a marriage could rock the very foundations of the relationship. They never admitted that the ups and downs could completely change the dynamics of the marriage and alter the couple's perspectives and outlooks regarding the other partner. These were all things that could cause a shift in a marriage, and just like a crack in a sidewalk left un-repaired, the shift can widen into a permanent chasm. In our case, the chasm widened by the day and I had to do something about it before I vanished into the abyss. I had to try to leap to the other side where I could see the promise of a better future.

After the very diverse and interesting conversations, responses, and reactions I got from my family and friends, I realized that none of it mattered. I knew what was best for *my* life. I decided to move on with my plan. The next step was to speak with my children about my decision. I wanted to tell them before I told Paul I was leaving. I carefully planned for us to have dinner at one of their favorite restaurants. We had a great time that night as we shared a wonderful meal and lots of happy laughter. After dinner, I gently broached the conversation about their father. I started by telling them I'd been unhappy with their father for a long time. I reminded them that they'd seen a lot of the ugliness between us and that at times, they'd been swept up in our fights by default. I explained that I stayed with their father because I wanted to keep our family unit in place. I told them that I sacrificed *my* happiness because I wanted more for them than I did for myself, but that it was now time for me. My oldest child started to cry while the others just looked very disappointed to hear the news. The last thing I wanted to do was to hurt my children as a result of my decision to break up the family.

However, to my surprise, once my children began to speak, the expressions and tears I feared were those of sadness or disappointment were those of joy. Each shared with me how they cried many times for me because of how they witnessed their father mistreat me. They believed I deserved better, but as young as they were, they also understood that only I could decide that I deserved to be treated better than what their father was capable of doing. One of my children fearfully shared that he wished many nights that his father would disappear. He didn't want to be the one to kill his father because of the hatred festering in his heart for him. I was taken aback by his words due to the disdain I felt for myself at that moment. I never thought about how staying in an unhealthy relationship so profoundly impacted my children. I gasped at the thought that had my child followed through on his hatred toward his father, he would have ended up in prison simply because I believed I had to endure such treatment all for the concept of "marriage" and keeping up appearances.

I immediately began to sob from a kaleidoscope of emotions. I was happy that I was finally leaving, but after hearing my children share their feelings, I was sad and angry that I hadn't left sooner. Children matter, their feelings matter, and I never took the time to talk to my children, I simply assumed that staying in a family unit regardless of the circumstances was the best thing to do. Believe me, I was wrong! I continued to let my children speak and they went on to share that I had their full support. They were happy and ready to help. I was very thankful to have their backing for the new journey I was about to embark upon!

The next day, I planned to tell Paul that I was leaving. Everything was ready for my departure. I rented a condo, found a job, and wrote a settlement proposal for him to consider. When he got home from work, I had dinner ready. I told him I wanted us to enjoy dinner together and talk. He agreed. During dinner, I pulled the proposal out of my purse and started reading aloud, "I, Madison Smith, being of sound mind, would like to end this marriage and file for divorce as soon as possible." It took him a minute to absorb what he'd just heard. He looked shocked and bewildered. I actually found his reaction surprising, considering that we slept in separate rooms and hadn't lived together like a married couple for years.

As I watched, Paul's reaction very quickly transformed from surprise to anger. He asked me when I planned to leave and when I said "immediately," he started yelling at me. He went on a rant telling me I'd never make it on my own, that no one would want me, that he was glad I was leaving, and that now he could be with the woman he truly loved. He went on to inform me that he'd been seeing his ex-girlfriend for years and was happy to know he was finally free to be with her. I just sat there and shook my head. At last, I got up from the table, grabbed my purse, and headed for the door. I refused to engage in another argument with this man. Whatever he had to say could be said through my lawyer. I was off to start my new life. When I got to the door, Paul's parting shot to me was, "Fuck you!" I looked back at him and responded, "No, fuck you," and then quietly closed the door behind me.

Truth Be Told, I never believed I could put myself first. I believed that it was my duty to put my husband and my children above all else, particularly above my desires. However, I now realize that by not putting myself first, I couldn't adequately claim the power of my role as a mother, wife, and a woman. I smothered my needs, expectations, and desires, which left me defeated, depleted, and pretending for so long that I had become a lifeless shell. **Truth Be Told,** starting over can be scary, but for me, *staying* was too hard and leaving to explore the unknown was exciting. The fear of staying with Paul was greater than the fear of the unknown. **Truth Be Told,** I have no regrets about my decision to end my marriage and leave my husband. I'm a happier, more fulfilled person because I found the courage to leave. I've finally rediscovered me!

CHAPTER NINE

Amber

I Lost Him

How could I be so stupid? I lost my man! I tried everything I could think of to keep him. Why wasn't I good enough for him? I didn't demand anything from him. I was afraid that if I asked him for more than he was willing to give I might lose him, so I never pressured him about anything. I wanted to be the perfect girlfriend so whatever he wanted to do, I did. How did I lose my man? Why did I lose my man? What did the other woman have that I didn't? Why did he choose her and not me? All I knew was that I needed him, I wanted him, and that I couldn't live without him!

Rick and I met at my cousin's Super Bowl party. It was an exciting time for me because my team finally made it to the Super Bowl! I was hyped, probably more hyped than most of the others at the party. I came prepared to cheer my team on to victory. I wore all my team paraphernalia—my football jersey, team hat, my socks with the team's log, wrist bands, team scarf, and gloves. Yes, gloves to wear in the house. Even my underwear represented my team's colors! I was ready and I was prepared! A few of the men commented on my wardrobe and actually made fun of me because they'd never seen a woman so serious about football, but I didn't care what they said about me, I was focused on my team winning! Some of the men who didn't know me went as far as to quiz me about my team and were surprised when I responded with the correct answers. They found out quickly that I could go toe-to-toe with any of them about football. I grew up with three brothers and they and my father treated me like one of the boys. If I wanted to tag along with my father and my brothers, I had no choice but to learn all about football, basketball, baseball, and almost any sport you could name. I didn't mind. It was fun hanging out with my brothers and learning about different sports.

The day of the party, I was really into the game. I was yelling and screaming at the television and cursing the refs for making bad calls. I was completely engrossed in the game. Rick was one of the men who were astonished that a woman could be so invested in a game of football, so he started talking to me. I wasn't really paying much attention to him and didn't realize he was hitting on me until the end of the night when he sat down next to me on the sofa and struck up a conversation. I wasn't particularly interested in him or in talking to him because my team had lost and I'd lost money on a bet. I wasn't in a good mood. I was quite annoyed at him because *his* team won and he was wearing this stupid victor's grin on his face. He was talking about his team's win when I finally jumped up from the sofa, hugged some of my friends goodbye, and left.

The next day, I got a call from my cousin who'd been at the party and who was a friend of Rick's. He called to tell me that Rick was really interested in getting to know me and had asked for my phone number. I hesitated, then told my cousin it was ok to give my number to him. Rick called me about twenty minutes later. I thought, "Wow, I must have really made an impression on him if he called me so quickly after receiving my number." We chatted for a bit and he asked if he could take me to dinner. I agreed and we set a date.

Unfortunately, our date didn't go as planned. His brother was supposed to go to the airport to pick up their mother, but he had a flat tire, so Rick had to pick up his mother instead. By the time Rick arrived at the airport to get his mother, drive her home, chat with her a bit, and then go to his house to shower and get ready for our date, it was 10 pm. Rick phoned to apologize for missing dinner and explained that his mother's flight arrived two hours later. I understood and accepted his apology, however, I told him that 10 pm was too late to go to dinner and suggested another day for us to get together. However, Rick insisted he had to see me. I was reluctant, but he pleaded until I gave in.

When he got to my house, he was empty-handed. No food, no snacks, nothing but a big appetite. He was only at my place for ten minutes before he announced how hungry he was. He said he only had a light lunch at noon and was starving. I couldn't help think that if he was so hungry, he should have picked up something to eat on his way over. Instead of telling him he could go to the nearest store and grab a bite, I opened my big mouth and offered to make us something to eat.

That was my first mistake. I should have suggested ordering something and have Rick pay for it. After all, he wanted to take me to dinner, not have me work as a short-order cook. I whipped up a quick and tasty meal—shrimp scampi, salad, and some garlic bread. He was certainly impressed! He cleaned his plate and asked for seconds. It's interesting now when I look back. I thought it was too late to go out to dinner somewhere, but I didn't find it too late to cook for him to make sure he had a meal. His expectations and my almost subservient willingness eventually became a pattern in our relationship. Despite having to cook, we did enjoy our time together. We talked late into the night getting to know one another. When he was ready to leave, we made plans to get together again soon. We also made a bet on the upcoming All-Star basketball game. If his team won, he could have whatever he wanted and if my team won, he had to buy me something from one of my favorite stores. After we shook hands on the bet, I wondered what I'd gotten myself into if my team lost. I wanted to change my mind but decided to stand confident in my team's ability to beat his.

A week or so later, Rick showed up on my doorstep unannounced, and said, "Pay up! My team won, and you lost the bet". I asked him what he wanted and he said, "I want you!" I wasn't sure what he meant, so I asked, "You want me? What do you mean?" He replied, "I want to make love to you". I started laughing, but he said he was serious. I stood there for a minute contemplating whether to pay up or not but, ultimately, I decided to honor the debt. We had sex and it was good, but he enjoyed it much more than I did. He asked me to perform oral sex on him and I did, but he didn't offer to return the favor. He busted a nut and left me hanging on the edge without giving a second thought to my pleasure. I wanted to cum too. Instead, I just lay there silent and disappointed. I couldn't help think, "This man cares only about himself." I couldn't come up with a single reason why I should keep seeing him, but I did.

We spent a lot of time together, but we never left the house. Rick came to my house and we fucked, then he would get up and leave. I wouldn't see him again until the next time he got horny and knocked on my door. I wanted more. I wanted him to treat me like his girlfriend outside the bedroom. I wanted to go out on a Friday or Saturday night to the movies, dinner, or out with friends like other couples. However, I didn't suggest that to him, of course. I stayed silent. I was afraid to speak up, but looking back now, I don't know why I was afraid to tell Rick that I wanted him to take me out on a date, but I wasn't afraid to share my body with him or indulge in all the nasty things he wanted to do in the bedroom. Why didn't I believe I was worthy of being more than his private whore? I didn't believe Rick was hiding our relationship. After all, I was the one who allowed him to think it was perfectly fine to come over unannounced anytime he liked and I never pressured him to take me out. He always arrived at my house hungry, expecting to eat, and yes, I fed him. Despite his selfishness, I was enjoying myself. I was enjoying his company and I was happy to have a "boyfriend" regardless of the function (or should I say, "dysfunction") of the relationship. I hadn't had anyone special in my life for some time. Now I had someone interested in being with me and it felt good. I had a man and I liked it.

I made the best of our time together. When we weren't fucking, we spent hours talking. Rick was a philosophical type of dude. Our conversations were always intense and thought-provoking. We challenged each other's thought processes, beliefs, and morals. We stimulated each other mentally and on the physical side, I satisfied him completely. On the other hand, he left me dissatisfied and frustrated, but typical of what would become my standard response, I simply suffered in silence for the sake of having a man in my life. Because we spent so much time in the house, we fucked like rabbits every chance we got, and eventually, I ended up pregnant—my first pregnancy.

We'd been seeing each other for about a year when it happened. The day I found out, I couldn't wait to tell Rick. I just knew he'd be as excited as I was! I called him to tell him that we really needed to talk— that I had something special I wanted to share with him. He said he'd see me later that evening. I was so happy and excited I couldn't sit still. I put together a special evening for us. I prepared a wonderful meal, set the scene with candles and roses, put on some great music, and carefully planned the surprise reveal that I was pregnant. Well, 7 pm came and went. He hadn't shown up by 9 pm, and he still hadn't arrived by 11 pm. I started to worry. Had something happened to him? Why wasn't he here yet? He said he was coming. Around 1am I finally fell asleep. I awoke around 3 am and checked my phone to see if he called or replied to my text messages, but he hadn't. The night was ruined. He stripped all the joy and anticipation from the evening and my exciting announcement.

TRUTH BE TOLD | ALETHEA TAYLOR

At 8 am the next morning, the front door
slammed shut and woke me up. It was Rick. As upset
as I was the night before, as soon as I saw him, I forgot
all about my anger and disappointment. He was here
now and that was all that mattered. He walked into the
house and looked around at the romantic set-up. He
asked, "What's up? What's this all about?" My joy and
excitement rekindled, and I answered, "I wanted a
special evening for us because I have some great news
to share with you." "What?" he asked. "What news?" I
grabbed his hand and told him that we were expecting
a baby. Rick's response certainly wasn't what I
anticipated. He was bewildered and mumbled,
"What...baby...?" "Who's pregnant?" I replied, "I am.
We are! We're pregnant!"

While I was smiling from ear to ear, he didn't
seem happy at all. I grabbed Rick's face, looked into his
eyes, and said, "Baby, we're pregnant. We're going to
be a family." He jerked away from me and immediately
told me that I had to abort the baby. I was confused.
What was he suggesting? What did he mean? He
wanted me to abort the baby? He looked at me and
said that I *couldn't* have the baby. I demanded to know
why. He said, "You can't have this baby. *I* can't have
another baby right now!" I tiled my head the way dogs
do when they're confused about what humans are
telling them. That's exactly how I felt—confused!

Rick sat me down and explained that I couldn't have the baby because he just had a baby a month ago. What was he telling me? Did I understand him correctly? Had my man just had a baby with someone else? He went on to say that he'd had a baby boy a month ago and that he and the mother had only had sex once, but she became pregnant and decided to keep the baby. I wanted to know why I was just learning about this baby, so I asked, "Why didn't you tell me you got another woman pregnant?" Rick's reply was typical of him. "Because it wasn't your concern. It didn't have anything to do with you, so you didn't need to know about it."

I was taken aback by his answer to my question about the baby, but I was totally astonished that he insisted I abort *my* baby. I wanted to keep my baby, too! This was my first pregnancy. It wasn't a mistake. We had unprotected sex so pregnancy had always been a possibility. I told him I didn't want an abortion, that I wanted to have my baby and that I wanted us to become a family. He told me if I didn't abort the baby, he'd leave me, and then he stomped out of the house. I called and texted Rick for more than three weeks but he never answered. I began to think maybe he was right. Now wasn't the right time to have a baby. I thought having the baby wasn't worth losing him, so I had an abortion without his knowledge.

Two months passed and I still hadn't seen or spoken with Rick. I continued to call but I always got his voicemail. I left him countless messages telling him I had an abortion and wanted to see him. Almost three months after he walked out my door, and one-hundred messages later, Rick finally came to see me. He assured me that I made the right decision and that now we could pick up where we left off. I asked him about his son. I wanted some details but he told me not to ask questions about his son if I wanted to keep seeing him. I changed tactics and asked him about his son's mother. He did tell me who she was and that they'd grown up together, attended the same elementary and middle schools, and that she lived on the same block where he grew up. They reconnected a couple of months after he met me, which was when his son was conceived. Rick assured me that he wasn't romantically tied to his child's mother. They were simply co-parenting and I had nothing to worry about. Of course, I didn't believe him. I never asked about his son again, but I made up in my mind that I was going to learn as much as I could about the boy's mother.

I became completely irrational. I wanted, no, I HAD to learn everything I could about Rick's "baby mama". I was obsessed with finding out all about her. After all, she was my competition. I hated that she had the attention of my man. I had to find out what was so great about her, what was so special. I had to get to know all about her. I had to make sure she wasn't romantically involved with Rick. I was convinced that the more information I gathered, the more ammunition I'd have to use to my advantage and successfully show him I was the one for him. I had to steal back his attention. I had to stop this woman! I was incredibly angry with her but for some sick reason, I wasn't angry with Rick. I felt she was forcing him to interact with her by using their son as leverage, so it was up to me to put a stop to it. My determination became an obsession.

I discovered her name and her home address. I visited her Facebook page, Instagram page, and looked her up on Snapchat. I copied every picture she'd ever posted, and then I learned all I could about her family, friends, and followed all of them on social media as well. I decided that she wasn't going to have Rick even if she did have his baby! He was mine and I wouldn't let her take him away from me. When I got her phone number, I called her. I told her I was Rick's woman and that she better understand that I wasn't going anywhere. We argued and threatened each other. She told me she had his child so I didn't have a chance with him and I retaliated by saying that he always came back to me and that I'd always be there for him. As far as I was concerned, she had interfered with my life and the plans I had for Rick and me. I wasn't going to let her completely destroy our lives.

As confident as I might have sounded when talking to her, I began to doubt myself. I questioned how I looked, how I dressed, how I wore my hair, and how I spoke. I decided that I had to do whatever it took to ensure I was more appealing than she was. I'd never see Rich without my makeup. I always ensured I was in sexy clothing that I knew would turn him on, and I fucked Rick every chance I got so he wouldn't want to have sex with her. I began trying to change everything about myself at the expense of the real me. My transformation started innocently enough but it quickly escalated.

Before I knew it, I didn't recognize who I was anymore. I had my butt enhanced, my breasts enlarged, my lips plumped, and vaginal rejuvenation. I started dressing differently by wearing designer clothes with no regard to expense. I did whatever it took to keep his attention focused on me. I knew what she looked like and was convinced that with all the procedures I'd done I clearly had an edge over her. Surely Rick was mine now. He seemed to like how I looked after my procedures. He loved the changes to my body, and he couldn't keep his hands off me. But he particularly loved my big new butt! I looked so good I thought he'd want to take me out and flaunt me around town in front of his friends. When I suggested that he take me somewhere, he said he didn't want other men staring at me and talking about me because then he'd have to knock someone's head off. Oddly, I understood that, so we continued to stay in the house and enjoy each other—and yes, that meant sex, sex, and more sex.

The year after my procedures, I discovered I was pregnant again. I was excited and again, I imagined that he'd share my excitement. His son was more than a year old now, so I thought by the time I had my baby, the children would be almost two years apart and easier for Rick to deal with than to have two infants at the same time. Once again, the first thing I did when I discovered I was pregnant was to call Rick to tell him I had something I wanted to discuss with him. However, this time, his phone kept going to voicemail. I left countless messages, but he never returned any of my calls.

About a week later, Rick finally called. I asked him where he'd been and he told me that he'd gone away for work and had forgotten his phone. He said he'd stop by later that evening. I never questioned him about not responding to me. I know it didn't make any sense, but I always believed what he told me. It didn't matter now anyway. I was too excited about my pregnancy and I couldn't wait to see him! Just like before, I prepared a special dinner and set the mood for a romantic evening together. When Rick arrived, he seemed very happy to see me. I know I was happy to see him. I jumped into his arms and gave him such a passionate kiss that we ended up skipping dinner and made love right there in the living room.

Afterward, we sat down for a quick dinner and then started to chat. We were both in such a happy mood that I knew this was the right time to tell him about the baby. I pulled the pregnancy test stick out of my purse and handed it to him. He looked at it and started shaking his head. I thought that was a good thing, but he looked at me and said, "We can't have a baby". I started to cry in confusion. I asked, "What do you mean? Why can't we have this baby?" Rick looked at me and said, "I got married. We just got back from our honeymoon. I love both of you, but she has my son and wanted us to be a family". I collapsed to my knees, my body spasming with sobs. I grabbed at his clothing, screaming, "Why, why, why would you do this? Why didn't you choose me?" He said he hadn't meant to hurt me and that he loved me, but he loved her more. She had his son and now she had him and they were a family. He finished by saying that we couldn't see each other anymore. I started screaming and shouting again. I told him to leave because I couldn't digest his words and I couldn't stand to look at him.

For a while, I looked at the world through a haze of shock and hurt. I couldn't believe the man I loved so much and who I thought loved me, had married someone else. I repeatedly played the scenario in my mind and heard Rick's voice with perfect clarity as he told me he was married. I beat myself up wondering why he hadn't chosen me. I tried to be everything that he wanted in a woman. Whatever he wanted me to be, I was. He had to have known that I was the best woman for him, the best choice, and that I was the only woman he'd ever want or need.

Sometimes he called me at three am to tell me he was coming over for a bite to eat and that he was bringing a couple of friends. It didn't matter if I was asleep. Like an obedient puppy, I got up and went to the kitchen to make a full meal for him and his friends. Often, he called me at five am when his shift ended to tell me he wanted a hot breakfast ready when he got home. I'd jump out of bed and practically run to the kitchen to prepare his breakfast, then hurry to his house and wait in my car for him to get home. I didn't have a key to his place like he had to mine, but I was more than happy to play the mindless servant and hand him a hot meal.

I bet that bitch of a wife never did those things for him! I was devastated! I wanted to die! The pain of losing him was too much! The sensation was like a knife piercing my heart, or that someone had reached into my chest and yanked it out. I couldn't breathe, sleep, or eat. The thought that Rick no longer wanted me, didn't want to be with me, was too much for me to handle. I became physically sick and all I could do was cry! So often I huddled in a fetal position and rocked myself back and forth for hours at a time. I wanted to wrap myself tightly enough that my body would stop shaking and the vomiting would subside. Though I wanted to stop myself from falling completely apart, nothing helped. I was so distraught I never noticed when I started pulling my hair out by the handful.

At first, it was just a reaction to my self-directed rage for being so stupid and losing my man. The collision of my rage, sadness, and hurt, coupled with the fear of living without Rick, manifested in ways I could never have imagined. The hair-pulling incidents escalated and I began biting the inside of my cheek. Then one day I picked up a razor blade and began cutting my arms—yes, I graduated to full-scale self-mutilation. It was an out-of-body experience. I couldn't believe I was cutting myself, but even as that thought filled my rational mind, I couldn't make myself stop. For some reason, cutting, in some small way, helped alleviate the horrific mental pain I was experiencing. It wasn't long before cutting my arms wasn't enough. I started cutting my thighs and cut so deeply that I bled through my pantyhose and pants. I used sanitary napkins to absorb the blood. Every time I saw the blood gushing from my flesh, I felt a moment of relief, but it wasn't enough. It was never enough. I wanted permanent relief from the pain of losing Rick. My mental anguish had become so torturous, so relentless, I finally attempted to commit suicide.

Instead of cutting my hands or thighs to ease the pain, I decided to cut my wrists and take some pills. I couldn't even get that right! I called my best friend to tell her that I loved her and asked her to tell my family that I loved them, too. She immediately knew something was wrong. She tried to keep me talking on the phone but I hung up and didn't answer when she called back. Because she knew something was wrong, she rushed over to my house. She had her own set of keys because she looked after my cat when I was away on vacations. She found me sprawled on the bathroom floor covered in blood. She started screaming at me, "Stay awake! Stay awake! You have to fight! You have to fight for yourself and for the baby, too." My brain was foggy, but I remember thinking, "Baby? What baby?" Oh, my God, I forgot I was pregnant! I was so sick about losing Rick and mired in self-pity, I forgot I was pregnant! My friend slapped my face hard and yelled, "You fight for this baby! Don't you dare die! You fight! This child needs a mother!" She called 911 and I was rushed to the hospital. I lived, but unfortunately, I miscarried.

My friend called Rick to tell him I'd been rushed to the hospital after an attempted suicide. He listened silently as she talked but he never responded or asked about the baby. That was typical of his behavior.

He never felt like he owed me anything, not even a moment's care or compassion. He showed no regard for me during our entire relationship. Why would he care about what happened to me now? He was confident I'd take his shit and not even think of walking away. But I surprised him this time. This was different. I lost my child because I couldn't deal with a man who didn't want me. An innocent child was gone forever—a child that I wanted but that I'd never had the chance to hold. I'd paid the price for loving the wrong man and trusting him with not one child's life, but two. The pain I now faced wasn't because I'd lost Rick. Now I'd have to live with the thought that I'd killed my child because of him. Yes, I survived, but my child paid for my stupidity and selfishness. The desire to die remained. I felt like I committed a crime so vile I didn't deserve to live.

I was committed to a mental health facility to get the help I badly needed with my suicidal thoughts. I can admit now that I needed that help and needed it desperately. I received 24-hour care, support, and counseling while I was hospitalized. It took quite a while for me to heal. I did heal-physically, but most of my time there was spent dealing with the demons in my head and the emotional instability that propelled me to the decision to take my own life. **Truth Be Told,** I lost myself and all sense of self. I wanted this selfish man more than I wanted anything else, even more than I wanted life. No matter how badly Rick hurt me, treated me, or disappointed me, I continued to love him. **Truth Be Told**, I *taught* him how to treat me. I'm the one who permitted him to treat me so badly. He simply became the student who simply followed what he learned from me.

Truth Be Told, Rick continued a pattern I established early in our relationship. He constantly blew smoke up my ass and like the fool I was, I accepted it. He never followed through on anything because I allowed him to get away with it. Since I set such low expectations for him, he felt no obligation to do more than I demanded. He knew he'd face no consequences for his actions, so he had no incentive to stop treating me like shit. Why should he change when the door was always open for him to come crawling back into my bed regardless of his appalling behavior?

Truth Be Told, the trouble was that I never believed I was good enough for him and my needy behavior demonstrated that. Rick had my heart and he knew it. Taking advantage of it was easy for him. As long as he knew I loved him more than he loved me, he had the advantage. Like a puppeteer jerking my strings, he did whatever he wanted and used me however he wanted. Looking back, I think he found my weakness unattractive. I don't think he ever thought of me as "the one". I thought he loved me, but maybe I never knew what love really was. He was a habit as powerful as any drug, and like many addicts, I had to hit rock bottom before I could claw my way back to recovery. I was powerless around him, but I learned a bitter lesson that it's *never* good to be that weak for anyone.

Truth Be Told, if I hadn't attempted to take my own life and, in the process, lost my precious child, I would have never sought the counseling I needed. While the chaotic events in my life were overwhelming to deal with, I found salvation in the counseling I was "required" to receive. At first, I was ashamed to tell anyone about it but it truly turned out to be a blessing in disguise. Through the help and support I received from the counseling, I learned to love myself and forgive myself for the mistakes I made in my life. **Truth Be Told**, I always struggled with feelings of inadequacy and "being good enough". I felt the need to prove that I was worthy of someone's love. I'm learning now that losing my mother earlier in my life to drugs and knowing she chose drugs over me left me with a sense of worthlessness and the belief that I didn't deserve love. However, through continued therapy and counseling, I've come to realize that more than anything else, I was *always* good enough. The real truth is, Rick was never good enough for me!

CHAPTER TEN

Iris

I Cry

"I hid behind a fake smile and laughter to mask my loneliness and pain. I was an actress playing an Oscar-worthy role, but secretly, I cried."

When I look back on my life, I remember being a vibrant, happy child and teenager with no reservations or insecurities. I remember rarely crying unless it was related to my parents either not getting me what I wanted or telling me I couldn't do something I wanted, so I was basically crying to get my way. However, by my early twenties, crying had become a daily habit. Somehow, I transformed from a vibrant young girl to a depressed, isolated young woman.

As a young girl, I was active and always involved in several different sports—soccer, track, swimming, and even rowing. I carried my enthusiasm for sports throughout my teen years and high school. I even landed a full-four-year college scholarship for rowing. Life was good. All I cared about was sports. I focused on studying and rowing and felt fulfilled.

However, everything changed for me one day during my junior year of college. I was invited to attend a party with some friends. After hanging out for a short time, I realized all my friends were snuggled with a guy, except me. It was a pivotal moment for me. I never thought about pursuing a relationship with anyone, but what was more alarming was that I couldn't remember when someone showed interest in me or even tried to ask me on a date. There was nothing. No one. Not even a passing flirtation.

That night spawned the beginning of my insecurity, self-doubt, and pervasive belief that I was undesirable. It was the first time I cried, but it would be far from the last. Somehow, the activities I enjoyed were no longer enough. I wanted someone to love me, to desire me, to be in a romantic relationship with, but my desires and reality never aligned. I graduated from college as a single young woman plagued by self-doubt, sadness, and tear-soaked pillows. And, I secretly cried.

Eventually, I did come to date a few guys after college, but nothing long-term or meaningful. I just couldn't seem to make a connection. Before I knew it, I was in my late twenties and single. Unsuccessful at finding a relationship, I began to doubt my self-worth and became susceptible to an increasing sense of isolation and loneliness. And, I secretly cried.

Everyone around me was in a relationship or

had a man in their life they could hang out with or turn to for needed sexual healing, but I didn't. I wanted to be in a relationship more than I wanted anything else. I was so miserable, but no one knew because I kept a smile on my face and pretended that I was happy being single. I wore a mask to conceal my feelings to the world, but inside, I struggled with the pain of loneliness and self-doubt. Why couldn't I find a man? Was there something wrong with me? There had to be a reason why I was still single.

I wanted so badly to spend time with a man. I dreamed of a Friday night when he'd come to my place for a night of us, to enjoy a bottle of wine, some good music, and laughter, but that special Friday never seemed to come. Instead, I was pressured to spend countless Fridays on a girls' night out. Once or maybe twice a month I joined some girlfriends for some fun. But after a while, I began to dread spending another evening with women who were either married or in a relationship. The conversation never strayed from their men, which defeated the purpose of going out with the girls. It was supposed to be about us, not men or kids, but a time for us to relax and have fun, but it never worked out that way. Even more upsetting to me was spending another night with women who continued to address each other as "bitches", as though it was a term of endearment. It's no such thing no matter how society tries to normalize it. I couldn't understand why women would think such derogatory terminology was an appropriate way to address each other.

It baffled me how two angry women calling each other bitches could escalate almost to a fistfight and a man calling a woman a bitch would be deemed disrespectful or even abusive. Yet, it was fine for women to use the word as a term of affection. I'd had enough, and the frustration made me cry. I didn't want to go to another movie, event, or bar with other women. I didn't want to listen to endless conversations about periods, the latest makeup, clothes, or shoes. I simply didn't want to do it!

I cried because I desperately wanted to be with a man. I wanted to be surrounded by masculine energy, a masculine body. I wanted a man who wanted me as much as I wanted him. I cried because I was tired of returning home and opening the door to my house and not smelling the scent of cologne or his clothes in the laundry hamper. All I smelled when I opened the door was the scent of my favorite perfume lingering in the air. I cried when I sat down to dinner and there was no one sitting across the table from me to enjoy our meal and talk about the events of our day. I cried as I prepared for my bath, complete with romantic candles, soft music, and a tub full of bubbles. Instead of sinking deeply into the warm water and enjoying the sensation of a man's strong hands caressing my body and scrubbing my back, I felt only the emptiness I carried back to my bedroom because there was no one waiting in bed for me, no one to make love to me, no one to hold me as we fell asleep.

I craved sex so badly it was a physical ache night and day. It was a hunger as debilitating as starvation. I longed to be touched, to be held, to feel a physical connection with a man. Sexual fantasies became my escape, and most nights I used toys to stem the throbbing in my vagina that resonated throughout every cell of my body. But they were only temporary fixes that left me only more bitter and frustrated. I cried because, in the morning, there was no impression on the pillow beside me, no one to make coffee or bring me breakfast in bed, no one to wish me a good day as I left for work. There was only sadness and silence.

It became a struggle for me to fight these emotions, but I fought as hard as I could to not let them win. I would attend different affairs and events hoping to meet someone and that the painful yearning in my heart would transform into a joyful, spiritual recognition when I saw his face. But to my dismay, that never happened. That's when I turned to dating websites and found Hudson.

Hudson and I attended the same college in Boston. Although I hadn't seen him since we graduated, I heard he was a successful architect. In college, we didn't hang out or were "friends". However, we did have a lot in common. We both were on the rowing teams. We both were vegans and sometimes would chat briefly when we would see each other at this vegan spot off-campus. But we never spent time together because he had a girlfriend. When I saw his picture on the dating site, I immediately sent him a message. He responded quickly and asked me out. I said yes, and we met that night for drinks.

When I first saw him, he looked even better than he did in his picture. Clearly, he was a man who stayed in the gym. He was gorgeous—6'4", muscles in all the right places, a beautiful head of hair, and a smile that melted me like a glacier. He bore an intoxicating smoothness, and if his physical attributes weren't enough, he was beautifully dressed in designer clothes. Every man I'd ever met paled in comparison to this Adonis. His aura exuded a masculinity that fueled a frenzy in my imagination. In my mind, all I could think was, *I want this man!* He greeted me with a warm hug, and the scent of his cologne triggered an immediate sexual response in my body. All I could fantasize about was how sexy he looked and how incredible it would be to have sex with him! I was so elated. I hoped that our night would go well and he would want to see me again. As the night progressed, we were having such a good time. It was clear that we had a connection!

I was happy but tried not to make it so obvious to Hudson. **Truth Be Told**, I felt he was my reward for the loneliness I'd endured, and I struggled to contain my tears. When it was time to go home, he helped me with my jacket and gave me another warm hug. I melted into his arms and felt I could live in his embrace forever. He walked me to my car but before I unlocked the door, he suddenly asked, "Iris, may I have a kiss?" I didn't hesitate. I leaned over and kissed him. The intensity of his kiss stunned me. I'd never experienced anything like the sensuality and passion of his lips, our tongues were in sync, and what we shared was the *perfect kiss*. It was overwhelming, incredibly satisfying, and unbelievably exciting. If it was a prelude for what was to come, I was in for the sexual experience of my life. When I returned home, all the emotions pent up within me burst like a dam. I cried, but this time, I cried tears of joy!

High from the afterglow of our date, I decided I wanted Hudson in my life. I couldn't stop thinking about our kiss! I even woke the next morning to sweet good morning greetings from him. I was so overjoyed to have someone interested in me that I cried with happiness! After our first date, we spent every day together. We were inseparable, and it felt so right. It came a time when I needed a physical bond with him, and I believed that connection would cement our relationship. With that agenda in mind, that became my goal.

TRUTH BE TOLD | ALETHEA TAYLOR

I remember the evening like I lived it every day.
Two months to the day of our first date, I planned a
romantic evening together, I cooked dinner, opened a
bottle of wine, and placed a pack of condoms in the
nightstand. When he arrived, we didn't waste any time,
the energy between us was electric. As soon as I locked
the front door, Hudson pulled me into his arms and
kissed me with such passion that all I wanted to do was
have sex with him right there. We spoke only through
our hands and mouths. I was so wet and excited I
could barely breathe.

I guided him to my bedroom. Every nerve in
my body pulsated with raw hunger. I wanted us to take
our time because I wanted to enjoy every moment of
the experience. His touch sent shivers through my
body, and as we undressed each other, I could only
stare in astonishment as his magnificent, sculpted body
and even more magnificent cock rising like a
truncheon. I didn't even know how he'd get it inside
me. It had been some time since I'd had sex, and I was
sure it was going to take some work for his cock to fit.
I think he could tell by the look on my face that I was
terrified by the size of his cock, so he focused on
calming and relaxing me. While he passionately kissed
me, I asked Hudson to get the condom in the
nightstand drawer and use it. He asked me why and
said we didn't need it. In the back of my mind, all I
could think of was how many women a man as

gorgeous as Hudson must have had and so I asked him about his previous partners. When he told he me he hadn't had sex in a while, I was shocked. I then asked if he had any sexually transmitted diseases. He replied, "Do I look like I have any diseases?" I said, "No, you look quite healthy". And then he started to kiss me in places that made me abruptly stop talking and relax and enjoy his sensual touch. I decided I'd ask him to put the condom on when we reached that point, but when we did, Hudson resisted.

He told me he didn't like condoms because he couldn't feel anything. He insisted that he was responsible and that I had nothing to worry about. While his reassurances didn't make me feel completely at ease, I was afraid to insist in case it put him off, so I didn't make an issue of it. As we fell onto the bed and I felt the weight of his body on mine, his hands and mouth melted most of my resistance, but I still felt uncomfortable as he entered me.

It wasn't so much his size. Hudson was extremely gentle and took his time, but my instincts still screamed from the depths of my mind. Hudson was my vision of the perfect man. He was a fantasy come to life and the answer to my prayers. At last, I had a man in my life. But I was having unprotected sex. I'd always been diligent about what went into my body. I hoped I wouldn't regret my moment of weakness.

TRUTH BE TOLD | ALETHEA TAYLOR

Thinking about Hudson the next day filled me with conflicting emotions. Our night together had been a blur of sex, passion, and complete satisfaction. I'd never felt such a sense of connection and fulfillment with any man. It would have been the most perfect evening of my life—had it not for my concerns about not insisting Hudson wear a condom. But when he called asking to see me again, I pushed my concerns aside. I wanted to keep feeling the way I did during our unforgettable first night together. We continued seeing each other throughout the next couple of months and having sex without a condom. I was more focused on no longer being single than I was about the consequences of unprotected sex.

As it happens, I was scheduled for my annual appointment with my gynecologist at the beginning of the year. During my appointment, my doctor asked if I was seeing anyone and if so, was I using a condom. Of course, I lied. I did not want to admit I hadn't been using a condom because she was a strong advocate for protected sex. She also asked if I wanted to be tested for STDs, which she did routinely. I decided to go ahead. I left her office confident that everything was fine—until I received a call from my doctor a little over a week later with the news that I'd contracted herpes!

When I heard her words, I immediately went into shock. My heart hammered in my chest, and I struggled to breathe. A few months earlier I struggled with loneliness and isolation, but now I was dealing with something that would forever change my life. I allowed my emotions and desperation to rule my common sense. Not only did I have to face the consequences of my actions, I also had to face Hudson. It was time to remove my rose-tinted glasses and look at the cold, hard facts. He hadn't been honest with me. Nor had I been honest with myself. I wasn't sure who to blame more. The tears I'd shed in the past had returned with a vengeance. I cried from the depths of my soul. I cried a river of anger and hopelessness, but I had to make sure no one heard me, so I secretly cried!

I didn't have the strength to call Hudson or confront him in person. All I could do was go home, crawl in bed, and cry. I didn't know how I could live with the consequences of my carelessness. How could I have trusted him so blindly with my health? I replayed the evening over and over again in my mind and cried. I screamed into my pillow until I fell into an exhausted sleep. I cried so much that I had no tears left to shed. By then, it was early evening the next day. I'd been in bed twenty-four hours from the time my doctor had delivered the news and I still had not spoken to Hudson. When I finally checked my phone for messages, he'd texted and called me multiple times, but the thought of him, the mere sight of his name popping up on my phone made me want to kill him! All I could wonder was why he'd do something so terribly irresponsible to me. But the greater question was why I'd do this to myself! I still couldn't muster the courage to call Hudson, so I let another day go by without talking to anyone.

Two days later, I texted Hudson and told him that I'd been sick but needed to speak with him as soon as possible. He called me a few minutes later. I didn't waste time with pleasantries and immediately confronted him. To my surprise, he admitted it was possible he had herpes but wasn't sure because he had no symptoms and hadn't been tested. I was in shock because I expected him to lie. He emphasized how he diligently maintained a healthy lifestyle. The silence at the other end of the phone bore into my soul. Though he spoke, I didn't hear his words. My illusions hung in tatters around my heart. I hung up and broke down.

Regret poured from the tears stinging my eyes. I couldn't believe I had an incurable disease. I'd acted like a stupid teenager mooning over her first crush. Instead of loving myself enough as a single woman and empowering myself, I became so dependent on the vision of being a couple, I lost myself in the process. I viewed myself as incomplete, an outcast, a hungry child staring longingly into the window of a candy store. I was envious of those who had love in their lives and lived vicariously through their emotions and experiences. I'd betrayed myself and my well-being for a fantasy.

As I cried, I grieved for the possibility of future relationships. How would I find a man now? Who would want to be with a woman who had herpes? It had been a struggle as it was to find someone, and when I met Hudson, I believed my prayers had been answered. Now, I was dealing with a burden. I didn't know where to turn or who to confide in. I could already hear the anger and disbelief from my family asking how I could have been so naive and careless. They always believed there was a reason I was single. Now I'd never hear the end of it. It was too much for me to deal with and over the next two weeks, I holed up in my bedroom. My family and friends called, but I texted them that I was busy. I never heard from Hudson again, which fueled my devastation. I didn't intend to stay with him or gain any strength from him, but I thought he'd at least have been man enough to apologize. I can only assume he was on the hunt for his next victim. I stayed in bed, depressed, and unable to function.

Finally, after a little over two weeks, I pulled myself together because I had to return to work. I may have been there in body, but my mind was in a different place. Three days after returning to work, even the simplest task proved a challenge. I could barely concentrate, and I realized I was spiraling into a dangerously dark place. How could I live like this? What future did I have? Would I be enslaved by medication to control the disease? Panic overwhelmed me. I felt hot and cold and began to hyperventilate. The last thing I wanted was my co-workers to notice my distressed behavior. I rushed to the bathroom and locked myself in a stall. Once again, the tears came. Racking sobs followed until I gasped for breath.

I almost missed the soft knock at the stall door. "Are you okay?" I recognized the voice of a co-worker I sometimes went to lunch with. I raised my head and stared at the door. She told me she was worried about me and asked if she could pray for me. I had a bottle of pills in my hand that I planned to take because I didn't know how to keep going. I didn't answer her, but I knew she could hear me crying. She knocked again, and asked, "Iris, may I please pray for you?" Again, I didn't reply. I heard her walk away and thought she was leaving, but to my surprise, she'd locked the main door to the bathroom and returned to the stall. Very quietly, she started praying.

She asked God to help me and give me what I needed to get through whatever pain I was dealing with. She said she was pleading to God on my behalf to resolve my issue, but if He decided not to fix it, to give me the strength to endure. I didn't want to come out of the stall, but as she prayed, I suddenly felt the comfort of arms wrapped around me. I exhaled. Clarity settled where despair had lived only moments ago, then calmness, and finally resolve. Why shouldn't I be okay?

Ending my life wasn't the answer, nor continuing to live in a state of misery and defeat. Why did I have to put myself through more torment? I'd already subjected myself to enough turmoil in my life. All I had to do was keep getting up in the morning and push forward a step at a time, which I'd been doing already. I simply hadn't realized I was pushing forward and choosing to live. Even though I cried daily, I was moving forward. I was living.

Now, I cry from gratitude for that simple knock on the stall door. I'm thankful for an angel disguised as my colleague who later became my friend and confidante. She allowed me to express my fear of being judged, ostracized, and shamed. Above all, I'm grateful for the strength that welled up from a source I never knew I possessed and the acceptance that compelled me to share my story because I know other women live with the secret shame of this disease. I learned to courageously step into the light to encourage other women and tell them they have the strength to make it.

Truth Be Told, I cry now because I hope other women will learn from my mistake of not valuing my body enough to protect it. I want them to understand that they should never allow the yearning for love to control their judgment and lead them to make reckless and dangerous decisions out of fear of losing a man and being alone. I've learned an important lesson that if someone loves and cares for you, they should protect you from harm, but ultimately it was my responsibility to protect myself.

I cry now in the hope that men will learn and understand that women aren't faceless victims to be used and discarded. We're their sisters, mothers, and daughters. Sex is supposed to be something sacred between two people. Instead, it has become a tool to destroy and disrupt lives, be it through the transmission of disease, sexual violence, or trafficking. While men may not have had or currently have role models to guide and teach them, that doesn't automatically strip them of the ability to know right from wrong and to treat women as less than human beings. I cry because I wonder how Hudson would have felt if a man had given the disease to his mother, sister, or aunt knowing he was infected but disregarding their lives and futures.

I cry now because I'm grateful for the support of a wonderful doctor who educated me and connected me to excellent resources and support groups for women. I thought love was impossible for people with herpes, but there are affected men and women looking for love. I cry now because there's hope!

I cry now because I realize crying is a necessary process to release, cleanse, and purge the heart and soul. I encourage my sisters to cry alone or with others and release the pain. And when the tears finally dry and you catch your breath, raise your head and take one step at a time toward your future. Love still awaits you!

TRUTH BE TOLD | ALETHEA TAYLOR

Truth Be Told, no more Oscar-worthy role for me! The mask is off. The tears have stopped, and now I raise my face to the sun.

CHAPTER ELEVEN

Zofie

I Imprisoned Myself

I thought his incarceration meant that his life was on hold, but I soon discovered that my life was the one hold. I altered my life for a man who didn't value me or the sacrifices I made for him. I was true to this man, but I can't say he was true to me.

I remember it like it was yesterday—that hot afternoon in the courtroom—the day my man was sentenced to eight years in jail for a crime he didn't commit. He thought if he told the truth about being in the car the night of the deadly shooting the court would be lenient and sentence him to no more than two years, but that's not how it turned out. Instead, James was sentenced to eight years. How could he be so stupid going anywhere with his fake ass, wannabe, dope-slinging, pill-peddling, in-and-out of jail, worthless excuse of a cousin? I hated his cousin because it was only a matter of time before James got caught up in his shit. I begged him not to hang out with his cousin, but he wouldn't listen to me. As a result, the police put chains on his wrists and feet and he was hauled away for something he didn't do.

When the judge banged the gavel after sentencing James, I was numb with shock. I sat there listening intently until I heard the judge say, "Eight years, Mr. Green." I heard this loud screech and vaguely realized it had come from me. Tears streamed down my face and I felt this unpleasant rush of anxiety flood my body. My insides were shaking, and I wanted to puke, pee, and shit all at the same time. I felt dizzy, nauseous, and my heart was hammering so fast I thought it would jump out my chest. The discomfort got so severe I thought they'd have to carry me out of the courtroom on a stretcher. That's how sick I felt.

James turned to look at me. I reached out to touch him but two guards jerked his body away from me and escorted him out of the courtroom. I was so angry I wanted to fuck James up and kill his cousin. I was angrier at James because of how stupid he was. It was his cousin's fault that he was heading to jail. I was devastated! My brain became a fog. I couldn't see or think straight. What was I going to do without James for eight long years? It felt more like eighty. My anxiety skyrocketed every time I thought of my man handcuffed.

I needed something to calm me down. I needed a drink. Then I thought, "No, I need a hit of weed to calm me down". Without even thinking, I reached into my shirt and pulled out some weed I had stashed in my bra between my breasts. As I absentmindedly put the pipe to my lips, my friend quickly snatched it away and asked, "What are you doing? Are you stupid, too?" I was so blindsided by what happened to James I only just realized what I was about to do. They could have locked me up for smoking marijuana in the courtroom. Then who would have been the stupid one?

Truthfully, I didn't care. All I could think about was James. I loved that man, and we were planning to get married the next year. We were going to buy a house, have a baby, but I told him that until he married me, I wasn't planning on having any kids. I didn't want to be a baby mama. We had to do things in the right order by getting married and buying a house. We were on the right track. We'd both worked hard to save enough money for our wedding and a down payment on our first house. We were so excited and happy until he made that disastrous decision to go with his cousin instead of going to my brother's party with me. My emotions were in turmoil. My head was spinning and I felt completely bewildered. My man was being taken away from me. My future was on hold. In a matter of minutes, my entire world had been turned upside-down.

James had never been to jail. He was a good guy who just happened to hang out with the wrong group of "boyz" who were all good-for-nothing losers.

TRUTH BE TOLD | ALETHEA TAYLOR

James was old enough to know that hanging out with these jerks could land him in a bad situation, but he never stopped to think that he could be found guilty by association. I knew because I'd learned about legal matters from watching all the cop shows on TV. The only good thing about being friends with those boyz was the protection they offered. His friends had reputations for being killers and they knew a lot of men who were already in jail. All they had to do was to put out the word and they'd make sure James was safe. He wasn't scared to go to jail or afraid of the people inside. He could hold his own but having brothers instructed to watch out for him was a bonus.

James was just disappointed in himself and unhappy that he was ending up in the one place he swore he'd never go. Knowing he was so unhappy, I wanted to do whatever I could to help cheer him up. I was one of those ride-or-die type chicks. If my man was hurting, I wanted to fix it. If my man was sad, I wanted to make him happy. If my man didn't have something he needed, I did what I could to get it. So, when my baby was locked down, I knew I was going to do whatever I could to help him get through his jail time.

As soon as James could receive visitors, I was there. But I barely recognized him. It was hard to get him to smile or make him laugh. He was angry with himself and regretted not going to the bar with me that

night. I pointed out that he couldn't do anything about
the past and had to focus only on the future—our
future together—but nothing I said seemed to work.
Seeing how miserable James was broke my heart. I felt
guilty when I laughed or found myself having fun or if
I didn't think about him every minute of every day. I
constantly checked myself whenever I enjoyed myself
in any way and questioned how I could be so
thoughtless when he was stuck behind bars without the
freedom to do what he pleased.

For the first year, I visited him faithfully every
Saturday. The drive to the prison was 3½ hours one
way, but I was committed. My family thought I was
crazy for visiting him every Saturday. They said I was
missing time with family or hanging out with my girls. I
worked all week, went to the prison on Saturdays, and
Sundays, I worked a part-time job cleaning office
buildings. There was never any time left for me.
However, I didn't care. All I cared about was seeing
James. There was no way I was going to abandon him.
I missed him so much and seeing him was the only
thing that helped. He was my priority whether he was
in prison or not. That's simply how I felt.

At some point, James began to worry I'd find
somebody else while he was in jail. That broke my
heart. I tried to reassure him that I loved him and only
wanted to be with him. Yes, there were a lot of
interested men around, especially those from the

neighborhood who knew James was locked down, but they didn't have anything to offer that would tempt me to break my commitment to James. No way was I hooking up with another man and end up disappointed. I was waiting for my baby to come home to take care of me. I assured James that my love for him wouldn't change because he was locked down.

To show how much I loved him, I made sure he had everything he needed. I put money on his books so he could buy things. I sent care packages straight from the prison vendors. I accepted all his calls no matter the time, and I wrote to him daily. I wanted to make sure I provided all the support James needed, so I stayed focused on him and him alone. Don't think I didn't have physical needs. I *wanted* to have sex. I needed to be held, to feel the comfort of being in the arms of a strong man, but I never tricked with anyone. I was waiting for James. I admit there were times when I was weak and felt like I was losing the battle against my physical needs and loneliness.

When that happened, I pulled up a picture of James on my phone, got out my purple dildo, thought about James' dick, and pleasured myself. That took care of my need for an orgasm and all was well until the urge returned. I told James that as long as I had batteries, he had nothing to worry about, but he wasn't convinced. I didn't know what else I could do to reassure him. He was very insecure. He pictured me out in the streets having fun, laughing and joking, and shaking my ass with men in bars. To please James and make him feel better, I stopped going to bars. He didn't want me hanging out with my girlfriends because he didn't want any of their boyfriends to bring a friend for me. He persuaded me that I didn't need to go out to have fun, that I could have fun in my own place, so I stopped hanging out with my girlfriends. I stayed home. All this made him feel better, but the more I stayed in the house, the more I drank to cope with my new reality and the more weed I smoked to numb the pain of missing James so much.

Despite all my efforts, they weren't enough to make James feel better. He knew I had close male friends and that we did a lot together. These were friends I hung out with. We drank, smoked, and partied together, but we were only friends. I was like a sister to them and they were like brothers to me. One day when I was talking to James, he told me he didn't want me hanging out with my male friends while he was away, so I agreed. Later, he added that he didn't want me talking on the phone with my male friends. He decided that talking with them would lead to sleeping with them. Again, to make James happy, I cut off all communication with my male friends. I was getting depressed. Regardless of what I did, I couldn't please James or make him feel secure about me. Little by little, by doing what he asked, I locked myself away. I put *myself* in jail.

My girlfriends noticed that I stopped hanging out with them and that I wasn't doing anything outside the house except work and visit James in prison. They felt like I was isolating myself and told me I really needed to get out of the house sometimes just to have some fun. They didn't hesitate to tell me that they thought I was stupid for listening to James. They also thought I should have some male companionship— someone to hang out with, someone to take me to dinner, someone to talk to, someone I could call when I needed sex. Like a martyr, I rejected all their suggestions. I didn't want to meet anyone else. It didn't matter how lonely I felt. What I needed was insignificant. All that mattered was James. I wanted him to feel secure and not worry about me on the outside. **Truth Be Told,** I was living like I was under house arrest. I left the house for short periods but had to be back home by curfew. I went to work and came straight home where I waited like a trained dog for James' phone calls, and then went to bed. The next day I repeated the same routine. I didn't recognize that I'd stopped living, but that's exactly what I did.

Thank God for good behavior! James only spent three years in jail. I can't tell you how happy I was when I first learned that he was being released years sooner than expected. I prayed a lot for James' early release, and I believe God heard my prayers. Grandma always said, "Take your troubles to Jesus. Just call him on the mainline." I didn't know specifically how to call Jesus on the mainline, but I did know how to pray out loud hoping God would hear me. I guess my Grandma was right. She always said God would help, and God did by releasing James from prison. I was so happy! I couldn't wait to see my baby and celebrate.

The day he was released I waited for him outside the prison walls. I remember it like it was yesterday. When he walked into the sunshine, I ran to him and jumped into his arms. I was rushing James and tried to get him into the car so we could go home, but he kept asking, "What's the rush?" I couldn't believe my ears. He had to know why I was rushing. My body needed him. He had some work to do. I wanted dick! I think we only made it three blocks before we pulled over and had sex on the side of the road. I had to have him and wasn't about to wait 3½ hours until we got home. Hell, no! The pit stop was brief because James came so fast, but that was fine. It was enough to hold me over. When we got home, we had sex all day and all night long. My boo rocked my world and I was ecstatic! I had my baby back home and nothing could have felt better, but unfortunately, my happiness didn't last long.

TRUTH BE TOLD | ALETHEA TAYLOR

After being apart for three years, I expected James to glue himself to me. I thought we'd spend every day together catching up on the sex we missed. Instead, for the first month after his release, he spent his time running the streets. I didn't complain because I realized after being behind bars for three years, he needed a little freedom. He stayed out all day and came home late at night. We really didn't spend much time together that first month. We slept in the same bed, but when we were awake, we were apart. After a month of allowing him to run free, I demanded that he start spending more time with me. He'd been away so long I thought it was time for him to start acting like a man in a relationship, a man who was planning to get married. He agreed but continued to stay out most of the time.

One night he came home late. He was drunk and his friends had to help him into the house and onto the couch. I left him right there and went to bed. At some point during the night, I got up to check on him and noticed he seemed to be sweating so I decided to take his off clothes so he'd be cooler and more comfortable. When I removed his pants, some things fell out of his pocket. To my shock, one of the items on the floor was a condom. I couldn't believe what I saw. A condom? Why did he have a condom? We didn't use condoms so why did he need one? I ran into the bedroom. My mind was racing, and I felt hot tears stream down my face. I was baffled, but then I paused and tried to calm down.

Maybe I had jumped to a wrong conclusion. Maybe the condom wasn't his. Maybe it belonged to one of his friends. Deep down I knew differently. I mean, why would a grown man carry a condom for another man? I didn't sleep at all that night. Instead, I contemplated how I intended to handle this situation. I decided that I wouldn't let him know I found the condom. I wanted to see what he had to say for himself. The next morning, he apologized for coming in late and drunk and said he wanted to spend the day with me. I'm not sure if he decided to spend the day with me so he could monitor my behavior (in case I'd seen the condom) or because he felt guilty about running the streets and thought it would be best to stay home for a change.

We had a great day together. We enjoyed each other's company and I never let on about the condom. I kept my cool until later that night when we were in bed. James was sleeping and I was watching TV when suddenly a text message chimed on his phone. I pretended not to hear it. I wanted to see if he was going to grab the phone to read the text or ignore it, but he was asleep. I eased out of bed, slipped his phone off the nightstand, and took it to the bathroom. The text read, "I missed you today". I thought, *Who the fuck is texting my man this time of the night? Who's texting him that*

they missed him? I texted back, "Who is this?" The
person responded, "Baby, it's me, Latrice."

Enraged, I picked up the phone and called her.
When she answered, I told her I was James' woman.
The woman on the other end of the phone insisted *she*
was James' woman and that he never mentioned he had
someone else. "What? Woman, what the fuck?" I yelled
into the receiver. I was shocked to hear this woman tell
me she was James' woman. I asked her how she could
possibly be his woman since he'd been locked up for
three years and had just gotten home a little over a
month ago. She told me she met James *before* his
incarceration and that she visited him the entire time he
was away. They picked up right where they left off as
soon as he came home. I told her that I was his fiancé
and that we were planning to get married. She said she
didn't care. She loved him and he loved her, and she
wasn't letting him go no matter what!

I was completely blown away by what I heard. I
couldn't believe it! This man that I'd been faithful to—
that I had put my life on hold for—had been cheating
on me while he was locked up, and as soon as he got
out, he ran back to her. At that moment, all I could
think was, *How the fuck does a man have the balls to cheat
while he's in prison? Seriously?* I talked with the woman for
well over an hour and asked her to come over because
I wanted both of us to confront James. She agreed. If
what this woman was telling me was true, I had to

question James' love for me and our plans to get married. I needed to know if he was really committed to our relationship and our future.

When Latrice arrived, James was still asleep. When I saw her, I was shocked. She could have been my sister. We definitely looked like we were related. We both saw the similarities immediately. While it was upsetting to find out about each other, we giggled and shook our heads because we truly could see why he was attracted to both of us, but of course, that didn't make it right. I had Latrice follow me down the hallway and asked her to wait there while I woke James. I told her to come in if he started to deny knowing her. We both approached the bedroom door, but she stayed in the hall while I entered the bedroom. I walked over to the bed and gave James a kick that rolled him off the bed and onto the floor. I demanded that he tell me who Latrice was and told him that he'd better not lie to me! He started yelling, "Why'd you kick me off the bed? I don't know what you're talking about!" I put my hands on my hips and said, "I'm talking about Latrice. I'm asking you about Latrice. Do you know her?" He said, "Yeah, yeah, I know her, that's…" I put a hand up to stop him and said, "If I were you, I'd think very carefully before lying to me. I'm only going to give you one chance to answer truthfully." He proceeded to say, "She's Brian's girl."

TRUTH BE TOLD | ALETHEA TAYLOR

Before I could utter a word, Latrice rushed into the room with her phone in her hand and said, "Brian's girl? *I'm* Brian's girl?" She shoved her phone in his face. The screen displayed a picture of them hugging each other in bed. They'd taken selfies. James was in complete shock. He asked, "What the fuck are you doing here?" She replied, "Hey, why do you care? You don't know me, I'm *Brian's* girl. Strangely enough, you're the same man who, just a day ago, had his face between my legs telling me how good my pussy tasted. Do you remember that, or do I need to pull up the video on my phone?" I reached over them and punched James in the eye. He fell back on the bed, but as I rushed to hit him again, he grabbed my arms and wouldn't let go. When I was finally able to jerk away from him, I warned him he'd better tell me the truth. I asked, "Is she your woman? Are you having a relationship with her?" Latrice chimed in and said, "You better tell her the truth!"

Finally, he admitted everything Latrice had earlier said was true. He said that he was sorry and that he never meant to hurt me and that he loved me. He went on to explain that he loved both of us and that it had been impossible to let one of us go. He had the audacity to ask if we could share him because he wanted both of us in his life. I stood there for a minute just staring at him. Beside me was my vanity where I kept my expensive perfume. I looked at him, grabbed a bottle of Chanel, and threw it at his head. The bottle found its target right above his right eye. Blood gushed everywhere. I glared at him and told him he'd better not think about putting his hands on me because I could have him locked up just by making one phone call. The motherfucker was on probation and I'd make sure he went back to jail. Latrice, on the other hand, said she didn't mind sharing him if it meant she could have him in her life.

I was shocked and became physically ill. The same emotions I experienced in the courtroom three years earlier had once again returned and overwhelmed me, but this time I pulled myself together and ordered him out of my house. I thanked Latrice for helping me confront him, but I needed both of them to get the fuck out. I couldn't come to terms that my man, who'd been locked up for three years, who demanded I put my life on hold until he came home, was living behind bars like a single man. I gave up everything for James, but he gave up nothing for me!

James didn't want to leave my apartment even with the blood pouring down his face, but I kept threatening to call the police. I couldn't stand to look at him and I damn sure didn't want to hear anything else he had to say. I didn't even care if he bled to death. I really needed him to leave before I hurt him. All I could think about was taking the knife I stored between my mattresses and stabbing that motherfucker, but I realized he wasn't worth it! I would definitely find myself behind real bars instead of the invisible ones I created for myself.

I called on my friends to help me get through the shock of the night and the breakup. My heart was shattered. The betrayal I felt was physical pain. I couldn't sleep, eat, and I had to take a week off from work. My friends tried to comfort me and I was happy they came through for me despite how badly I treated them. I felt so guilty, angry, and ashamed because I put my life on hold for this man. Now all I could wonder is if he'd ever loved me or planned to marry me. His admission that he was in love with both of us and wanted both of us was only about him. What he wanted. What he needed. Never mind what I wanted or needed.

Only now do I understand that what we had was never real. James played me for a fool. I wasted my time and paused my life for him. And for what? Why did the love and commitment I had for James mean I had to surrender everything because *he'd* been stripped of his freedom? He hadn't been loyal to me despite everything I sacrificed for him before, during, and after his incarceration. I'd been so blindsided by love that I allowed him to use me for his own benefit. I had to have answers. I wasn't sure if it would help ease the betrayal, but I thought I deserved to know the truth.

After three weeks of ignoring his calls, texts, and knocks on my door, I decided to call him and arrange a time for us to talk. I agreed to meet him at a bar for a brief conversation. When we met, I have to admit my heart sank when I saw him. He looked good. I wanted to run into his arms and kiss him, but my pain bound me to my chair like shackles. We talked and I told how indescribable my pain was. I told him he had no idea what I sacrificed for him and how hurt I was. I asked him if he thought I deserved to be cheated on. He replied, "I didn't mean to hurt you. I didn't mean to fall in love with Latrice, but that shit happens."

Yeah, *that shit happened,* all right. He admitted he loved us both and didn't want to lose either of us. He begged me not to leave him and to give him time to think things over. Well, I'm sorry, but as far as I was concerned, he had three years to think things over and all he could offer was that he'd try to keep both of us. He, and I emphasize the "he", just needed to see if we'd go for it. I looked speechlessly at James. To hear him once again confess his love for another woman was a knife jab to my heart. I was tempted to smash my beer bottle over his head. Instead, I got up from the table and walked away with tears streaming down my face.

Truth Be Told, I imprisoned myself. I didn't need bars. I simply stopped living. I didn't value my life enough to live for *me*. **Truth Be Told**, I thought I was the answer to James' happiness, that it was my responsibility to make him happy, but I had it all wrong. It was my responsibility to make *me* happy, and I could only do that if I was willing to live a full life, not like someone's puppet. **Truth Be Told**, James was living a full life behind bars while my life was on hold. He didn't stop seeing and engaging with people, but I did. He didn't choose me over all else, he chose himself. **Truth Be Told**, as I told James so very often, "You can't look back and change the past, but you *can* look to the future and learn from your mistakes." I've learned so much from my relationship with James. I'll never again put my life on hold or put a man's happiness before mine. Now I understand that living the way someone else dictates isn't living at all, but that *LIVING* is putting myself and my happiness first.

CHAPTER TWELVE

Samantha

I'm Ready for You

I wasn't ready to step into another relationship. I wanted to wait until the time was right. So many well-meaning people tried to persuade me I needed to find a man, that I had to have a man—but I knew I wasn't ready. I didn't want one—not until I decided I was ready.

I'm ready now. I'm ready for you now because I've had time to work on me. I had to learn to love me before I was open to you. I had to love every part of me, every part of my body that was unique to me, and that included my ass, which God created exclusively for me and shouldn't be compared with any other woman's ass. I needed to love my eyes so I could talk to you without worrying about whether they were the right color. I needed to love my nose because without it, how could I appreciate the special scent that is you? I didn't want to worry about its size, or if it was aesthetically pleasing enough for society to accept. I wanted to love my lips, not because they happened to align with current social media criteria that required injections to inflate them, but because they were perfectly shaped for my face and because they would, someday, softly touch and gently caress your lips and open just enough to let my tongue slowly emerge to confidently meet yours. I wanted you to enjoy my kisses that were sensual enough naturally.

I wanted to love my breasts because they're perfectly proportioned for my frame and primed for you to grab and lick. I didn't want to worry about their size, whether they were big enough, or to debate the dubious merits of implants. I didn't want to compete with a woman whose cup size was larger than mine. I wanted to love my vagina because it's a precious jewel and responds perfectly when she receives the arousal she needs. I won't worry that something is wrong with her because, for the right man, she'll awaken and purr and secrete just as she should to prepare for entry like a well-oiled machine. I wanted to love the skin in which I'm wrapped and honor every scar, every flaw, the tone, the complexion, and every imperfection because if I wasn't comfortable with the unique beauty that characterized me from all other women in the world, how could I expect you to love the radiant reflection of who I am and how I carry myself with such pride?

I'm ready for you because I took the time to face and deal with my issues. I've learned that the sum of my relationships doesn't have to be the baggage I continue to drag around with me. I've unpacked those overweight bags, the suitcases are empty, and I now understand that whatever went wrong in my previous relationships were issues with each particular person. I cannot and will not hold one man accountable for another man's mistakes. I'm ready for you because I'm no longer afraid to try. I was afraid of being hurt. The very idea of exploring love with another man paralyzed me, but now I'm exercising my muscles and have learned to take relationships one step at a time until my footing feels secure and steady. I'm ready for you because now I k*now* what I want. I'm clear about what I need and the values I seek in others. These are the fundamental essentials that form the solid foundation of a relationship. The right values ignite attraction, and then, at the right time, and not a moment before because rushing opens the gateway to disaster, the chemical compounds unite and combust. I've experienced one too many explosions in my life because I rushed the process or missed some important steps.

I'm ready for you because I now know who I am. I'm no longer that frightened, insecure woman who allowed some men to convince me I was because they knew my suspicions about them were accurate and were afraid I would expose them. Those men deflected their weakness onto me by calling me insecure. Yes, I owned that lie, but no more!

TRUTH BE TOLD | ALETHEA TAYLOR

I'm ready for you because I'm finally confident about who I am. I can hold my head high! I'm proud, and I possess an undeniable sexiness, my walk demonstrates my confidence, and my beauty is both internal and external. It shines brightly like a beacon. I'm a woman who knows what she has to offer, and more importantly, I acknowledge and honor my worth.

I'm ready for you because I'm strong enough to stand alone. If you decide to walk away someday, I won't wither and die. I'm ready for you because I don't *need* you. I do, however, *want* you, and I now understand the difference between want and need. I'm ready for you because I know now that I can't love you more than I love me. Our love must be balanced. We both have to equally contribute to the relationship because anything less is not acceptable. I'm ready for you because I understand that you can't make me happy. That privilege is mine alone. I know that when we join together, our union should be the result of the joy, excitement, and energy embracing us because we've truly connected.

Truth Be Told, I'm ready for you because I love me—fully and completely. So, I won't look for you. Instead, I'll be patient and wait until the right you, finds me.

CONCLUSION

We can't control how truthful someone will be. However, we can control how truthful we are to ourselves. If we want to have truly fulfilling, meaningful, and loving relationships, we have to know what we really want, need, and desire. It sounds so simple, but if we're unclear about who we are or what we want, fulfilling relationships will continue to elude us like an ever-receding mirage. Relationships will merely exist, but they won't thrive. Many will wither and die along with part of our hearts. If we choose to live the way we want, we also have the *power* to choose relationships that fulfill our needs. We don't have to settle, but we need the courage to recognize and avoid the pitfalls so many of us encounter in relationships.

We also need the strength to step aside from convention, expectations, and fear. As women, we're conditioned to fear everything—being alone, being single, and simply not conforming. We face endless challenges that test our resolve and weaken us. "Why don't you have a boyfriend? Why aren't you married? Why don't you have children?" Bombarded with this endless litany of how we're failing as women, it's no wonder we jump at relationships, regardless of quality, like sharks jumping for chum. We're brainwashed to believe that without a man in our lives, we're nothing. Incomplete. Objects of pity. *Failures.* But all these attitudes do is instill in us a sense that we're only half of who we are, of who we could be, and that we need a man to complete us. It's the ultimate irony that many women only discover who they really are *after* a relationship.

The most powerful weapon and source of strength we, as women, can have is to love ourselves enough to uphold our values and desires. We can't and shouldn't expect others to make us happy. Only we have **the power to create our own happiness.** The women in this book traveled a journey of revelations, realizations, and hard truths because they finally faced themselves and their expectations in the mirror. It's painful to look for answers to our relationship issues. We're forced to take a hard, critical look at ourselves and admit that maybe it's not the other person's fault. A relationship is two people. Two minds. Two hearts. We share responsibility and must identify it, own it, and be brave enough to change whatever hinders our happiness.

The process begins when we start asking ourselves hard questions and looking for honest answers. Are you happy in your relationship? Are you getting what you truly desire from it? Do you believe your present relationship meets your expectations, needs, desires, and wants? If not, are you willing to stand strong and resolve to be true to your desires to improve your current and future relationships? Living in a state of denial, unhappiness, pretense, and misery, is not living. It's merely existing until we accept that we have the *choice* to do something about it.

Yet we still stay in relationships that tear us down, beat us down, and break our spirit. We teach people how to treat us and then get upset when they mistreat us. Think about it. You stay in a relationship with a man who repeatedly cheats on you. When you discover his infidelity, you're furious! You can yell, scream, cry, and threaten to leave until you lose your voice, but if you don't follow up with action, he quickly learns there are no consequences to his behavior. He doesn't need to change his behavior because you don't change yours. You play the victim, but you never seek justice. Unfortunately, like the women in this book, many cave into their partner's destructive behavior and allow them to dictate their lives and the relationship rules. If you don't acknowledge boundaries in your relationship if, you don't know what is and isn't acceptable, who's really to blame?

Take inventory. Then take action. Start by acknowledging how much there is to love about you. Take time to note what you love about yourself. Above all, stop comparing yourself to others. Real life isn't a filtered Instagram post. Celebrate your uniqueness.

These qualities are yours alone in the world. Why would you want to be like everyone else? Consider all your strong points. Consider your weaknesses and how you can overcome them to be your best possible self. Never change for someone else. Be clear about what you're looking for—relationship, friendship, or marriage. Put aside what society expects from you and focus on what you want. Write down your expectations and desires. Think them. Breathe them. Shout them out. If you want a meaningful relationship, a sex partner won't satisfy you. A quick, physical fix will only leave you empty and distract you from your true objective. Be brutally honest about your relationship objectives. Only you can define those. What are your "non-negotiables"—those standards you'll stand strong on and refuse to compromise regardless of who the man is. If he doesn't meet your "foundational pillars", which are critical for the relationship, he's not the partner capable of building the relationship you want.

Resist the temptation to settle. If God made good women, why wouldn't He make good men with the same values and commitment? If we accept destructive behavior, mistreatment, or values that aren't committed to or aligned with yours, is this person worth pursuing? Physical attributes fade or change. Money and material possessions come and go. When that happens, all that remains is a person's heart and soul. What's important to you? Speak your truth. Don't be afraid to stand by, stand firm, or elevate your expectations or non-negotiables. If you can't love, respect, and honor yourself, don't expect that from anyone else.

Keep in mind not every relationship works out the way you want or hope it will. When a relationship ends, there's only one way to look at it. Perhaps you weren't meant to be *his* blessing. It's not about your weight, appearance, or skin color. It doesn't matter how big your butt or tits are. It's not about hips, lips, or eyes. It's about connection. It's that mysterious connection, that undefinable attraction that does it for that man. Of course, physical attraction is important, but what evolves after that initial attraction is far more critical. STOP trying to change yourself to fit him. You were never meant to be the final piece of someone else's puzzle. We've all been there. You get caught up in the emotion and the high and easily overlook any red flags. But once we know better, we should do better. We're all driven by our emotions to some extent, but we also need to pay attention to our instincts and inner voices. They speak to us for a reason. Sometimes, tough decisions have to be made no matter how painful. We must set good examples for all the women in our lives because eyes are always on us. Young women look up to us. They observe the silent messages we send when we settle for less. Instead of inspiring to strive for something better, something mutually beneficial, we're telling them to lower their standards when it comes to a partner. Would you really tell your daughters, sisters, or friends to accept less than they deserve?

You may not know what a loving relationship is. You may have allowed your fear of being alone, your insecurities, doubts, and negative experiences to challenge whether there's even such a thing as a fulfilling relationship. Maybe you've watched too many movies and feel a truly loving, nurturing relationship is only fantasy. Just remember, when something seems impossible, **God is possibility.** When things look grim, **God is sunlight.** And when you feel there's no hope, **God is hope.** What that means is that the man you feel is your perfect partner *is* possible. Do you believe you're a good woman? If you do, you must consider why God would want anything less than the best for you. You don't have to settle! You **do** need to learn how to endure, trust, and believe that there are great men out there. Settling is never an option. The one true thing we can believe and trust in is God. One of my favorite scriptures tells us to, "Trust in the Lord with all thine heart; and lean not unto thine own understanding. In all thy ways acknowledge Him, and He shall direct thy paths" (Proverbs 3:5~6). Why not put your faith and trust in God rather than an unworthy man? Don't you feel you deserve more than pain, heartache, and betrayal?

TRUTH BE TOLD | ALETHEA TAYLOR

We are women. Hear us ROAR! We give life, nurture life, and then we turn around and throw that life away like we're throwing out the trash. **Choose you!** Build a support system. Surround yourself with women who allow you to be yourself—to be real. Surround yourself with women who will support and pray for you. Surround yourself with women who'll elevate you, who are strong and good examples. Surround yourself with women who don't mind sharing their stories, who aren't afraid to want more, and will offer a shoulder to cry on.

The most important thing to remember is that you can always choose the path for the better, for more, for truth, because truth is freeing. It's power, and truth is powerful!

ABOUT THE AUTHOR

Alethea Taylor is an entrepreneur, actor, and advocate for women and girls. She has built a credible reputation as a dynamic motivational speaker on the Women's Conference circuit. Committed to the advancement of strong, confident women and girls, she has dedicated much of her career to providing women of all ages with the tools necessary to succeed both personally and professionally.

Alethea's primary mission is to help young girls and women build their self-esteem and recognize the value they bring to the world around them.

Alethea holds a Bachelor's Degree in Business Administration and a Master's Degree in Education. She makes her home in Philadelphia, PA – affectionately known to her as "the City of Brother Love and Sisterly Affection".

Made in the USA
Middletown, DE
07 March 2020